AWAITING ARRIVAL

STEVEN JAEGER

Awaiting Arrival
Copyright © 2021 by Steven Jaeger

All rights reserved. No part of this publication may be reproduced or transmitted in any form or by any means, electronic or mechanical, including photocopy, recording, or any information storage and retrieval system, without permission from the author.

For information about permission to reproduce selections from this book, write to author@stevenjaeger.com.

First edition: 01 2022
Printed in the United States of America
ISBN 979-8-9864112-0-0

Book design by Steven Jaeger

To my kids,
John, James, Gloria

26 March 2336

Chapter 01

A soft rustling grew until the noise finally broke Rick's sleep. His eyes opened slowly. He lay quietly in bed and waited for the persistent sound to end. He knew the sound immediately: a letter being shoved under his door. He frowned, rolled over, and tried to go back to sleep. The only time mail was delivered in physical form was when someone had died.

He had gotten somewhat used to it over the years. However, with graduation not far away, the frequency of these letters had increased to one every two or three days. In the past, those who passed were rather obscure or no longer relevant. The most recent deaths, however, were people much closer to him and were becoming more difficult to deal with.

"I sure wish they would slow down with these letters. It kills the excitement of almost being done," said a soft, apologetic voice.

After three months of marriage, Rick was surprised by how much he still enjoyed hearing Jessica's voice. When he first began the screening process with the partnering program, he assumed it was an educated guess, at best, when it came to how they paired people. However, he didn't need numbers to tell him that she was the love of his life. He knew after the first thirty minutes of talking to her that he would only be happy if he had her.

"Alright, lazy bones, it's time to get out of bed and come eat breakfast," said Jessica as she tossed the letter on the floor next to him. She paused before leaving. "Sorry about the letter. I know you really looked up to him." She gave him a delicate smile. Her brilliant green eyes, accentuated by the light freckles on her cheeks and small nose, and her full lips made it impossible for him to feel too forlorn.

Rick sighed. Her words were all the hint he needed. He watched Jessica turn to walk away, her long red hair flowing behind her. She was muscular, yet still soft and womanly beneath her pajama shorts and tight shirt. She walked away with just enough wiggle in her step that he knew that she knew he was watching her.

Moving his hand along the wall of his bed, he felt for the button to open the clear lid that made up the top half of his sleeping cylinder. As the lid slid to his left, a wave of fresh air, filled with the aroma of eggs and bacon, washed over him. The sleeping chamber had no impact on him now since it wasn't slept in for a long enough period of time to be useful. However, those about to embark on a long term space mission were told to start sleeping in it a month before they left so they would be used to it when the time came to use it. It's been said, that when used properly, the sleep cylinder could extend a person's life by over 250%, though the chances of the user dying from external forces rather than old age increased the longer they were alive.

Rick swept his thick brown hair away from his blue eyes and raked it back with his fingers. A strong nose and a confident jaw line made him attractive to most, but not stunning. He was tall and had a muscular build that filled the sleep chamber snugly. The cylinder was cramped, to conserve space and resources, and he wasn't looking forward to sleeping in it weeks at a time. He sat up and stretched out as he reached down and picked up the letter from the floor. The letter was from Hope In Extended Planetary Exploration, though most people referred to it as Hype. It read:

> Dear Captain Rick Lanson,
>
> We regret to inform you that Professor Henry Dalton has passed away. Before passing, he left this message for you:
>
> Rick,
>
> Through the last several years I have had the pleasure of seeing you grow from a humble student to a proud and capable captain. The journey ahead of you will be difficult, but I have full confidence that you will be the most successful and skilled captain I have ever trained. Good luck to you and your crew, and remember to stay focused.
>
> Your friend,
> Henry

Rick picked up a small box from the floor of his closet and gently set the letter inside. This was the forty-third letter he had received. He was expecting this one, and because of how important Dr. Dalton had been in his training, knew it was likely the last he would receive before he left.

. . .

26 March 2336

"You ready to inspect the ship today? All you have to do is make a proper inspection and you'll be captain." Jessica always knew how to distract Rick on a day that started with bad news, and that task was especially easy today. The final inspection was not just for a new captain to assess his or her ship but for Hype to evaluate the potential captain's abilities that should have been attained in the last four years of training. If he made enough mistakes during his inspection, he could lose his chance at becoming captain. It was very rare that someone qualified for a second inspection.

"It will definitely be interesting to finally see the Titanic in person, and not just from pictures and diagrams," replied Rick. The Titanic had been built over the last four years and was so large that all the parts had to be sent into space and then assembled because it would be nearly impossible to launch from Earth. It was named the Titanic by the crew assigned to the ship. Not just because of its size and speed, but because if the ship "sank" after the two year mark in their journey they would not have the resources to return home and they would be too far away for anyone to rescue them.

Rick still had a lot of things he was nervous about other than passing the inspection. Much of the technology that was going to be used on their trip was still in the final stages of development. There would be a lot of information to absorb in the next two weeks before they left as they learned how to use the new and potentially unreliable technology.

"Jason told me the ship has been finished for over a week and they are using this final time for finishing touches," said Jessica. "He also mentioned that they've finalized the details of our mission, so we'll get the full breakdown before the ship inspection."

"Yeah, the news of new potential planets has been floating around for about a week. I'll be interested to find out more. It must have been good if they wanted to set a new target for us," replied Rick as he finished his breakfast. He savored his last bite of bacon. "I'm going to miss eating meat."

"Going mostly vegan will be tough at first, I'm sure, but we'll have fish from aquaponics, and hopefully we will be too busy on our mission to notice missing other meats. Plus, I have recipes to make fake meats. We wanted to have animals on the ship, but there was just no way to manage the animals humanely while in the sleep chambers." Jessica shrugged. "It will be okay."

"I know we will have things to do, but we both know there is going to be a ton of down time, time to remember all the food I can't have anymore. At least until I forget what it tastes like."

04 April 2336
Chapter 02

"For the past four years, we have been working to prepare for a mission that would allow us to extricate resources from another planet, in an attempt to help maintain life on Earth," bellowed Dr. Rodriguez, a sixty-three year old ex-Lieutenant. A chiseled jaw line, stern brow, and pure white hair in a crew cut conveyed his many military years. "We have already begun to see the fruits of our labor, as previous ships, sent out within the last two hundred years, have begun reaching their destinations. We are slowly gaining access to more rare-earth elements and fuels that were previously becoming scarce." Dr. Rodriguez paused and looked around the room. Three hundred people filled the seats in the large conference room.

To Rick, the majority of the people in the room seemed complacent, if not completely disinterested. He knew that for everyone, other than the seven members of his crew, this was not the first time he'd heard a mission briefing. The specific details had no major importance to the roles of most people here and many of them usually skipped these meetings. Today had been different, though, as Rick had noticed people being told that attendance at this meeting was mandatory.

Dr. Rodriguez sighed. "Truth be told, these missions have not proven as successful as we had initially hoped. The planets we have landed on so far have been very dangerous for us to work on and have yielded less resources than what is needed to be a long lasting solution. It's beginning to feel as though mining other planets is like putting a band-aid on a wound that needs surgery."

Rick could tell that such a grim tone was not standard for a mission briefing. All those who were disinterested before, were now watching intently, drawn to attention by his honesty.

"And then we found planet D-173. Distant observations are showing signs of a surface environment much more hospitable than any we have found before." Dr. Rodriguez pressed a button on the remote in his hand, and a projection displayed on a screen in front of the audience showing a planet with an earth-like surface. "But this isn't about resource extraction; this is about relocation."

People immediately began whispering to each other. Many were shaking or nodding their heads. Several hands shot into the air, but Dr. Rodriguez gestured for everyone to be quiet so he could continue.

"Before we get ahead of ourselves, let's break down the basic facts about the planet and our mission." He pressed a button and the image was replaced with numbers. "This planet is over 1000 parsecs away from our farthest space station, which means it will take over 3,000 Earth years to get there. So everyone needs to take a breath, because only eight of us here will ever have a chance to see it."

"Also, according to current resources estimates, we won't last more than 2,500 years. A growing scarcity of vital rare-earth elements, an ever-growing population, and uncontrollable global soil depletion have been clearly measured and are now stated as fact. The only way people will survive long enough to enjoy this new planet is if the ships we have already sent out find planets that have what we need to hold us over. And *if* we can survive that long, it's a long distance to travel and the equipment is delicate. There are plenty of ways for things to break, and even if the crew and equipment both make it there intact, we have never tested teleportation from that distance. There is no guarantee that we will even be able to do anything once they get there." Everyone was silent. Rick looked at the members of his crew who, faced with the reality of the mission, sat next to him, expressionless, trying to absorb the news they were given.

"Some of you may be thinking about how some peoples' lives are dedicated to digging up things from 3,000 years ago. The amount of history that will occur between now and then, there could be people digging up our things when the crew finally arrives. At this point I've heard all of the arguments and analogies, even accusations, that this is simply a political stunt. The ship was designed to go farther than we have ever sent a ship before. It will still do that, just even farther than we originally planned. The crew was planning on spending most of their lives on this ship and losing everyone they knew on Earth. That is still true, just now it will be their whole lives. We knew when designing the original mission that this ship was only ever going in one direction and that has only become more true. What if somehow all of Earth's problems would be magically solved by then, despite our best efforts at fixing things for the past two hundred years failing? Well, we went to the moon just to prove we could. It didn't offer us resources and we couldn't move there, but we did it anyway. If humanity doesn't need a new home by then, then we just call it a victory in exploration. The ship will be charting all of the deep space that it has within its sights. Don't underestimate how much value that has, regardless of Earth's circumstances in the future. This is a big picture mission, though it is simple enough in concept.

"The captain of this ship, Captain Lanson, assuming he passes the inspection, will start by doing a two year test run at full speed. This is a big bird. It will take about two weeks to get to full speed and six weeks to slow it down gradually. The crew will inspect the ship to confirm its integrity and then continue at full speed until they reach Shadow Space Colony to deliver supplies. These deliveries are vital to them. The crew will be providing them with a new, significantly larger teleporter, that will provide them access to much larger replacement parts for currently struggling or dying systems, as well as materials that will allow them to grow their space station in critical ways. A final inspection will be made of the ship while they are there, at which point, they are then to confirm that they are prepared for the remainder of the mission. They will then embark on the final stage of their journey, outside the reach of external resources.

"Every ten years, their time, the ship will be slowed down and inspected. This will be the only time they will be able to communicate with Earth, to give and get status updates. However, communication hasn't been tested from that distance, so there could be any number of factors that affect the speed or ability of communication.

"Other than that, they just land the ship and initiate communication with Earth. The whole process is almost entirely automated, so there won't be much they'll have to do." Dr. Rodriguez let out a sigh. His large frame paced in front of the crowd. "I'm obviously simplifying things since the eight of you," he looked at Rick and his crew, "will be the only ones maintaining a ship with over a football field of vegetation, and all the equipment needed to keep you alive for three hundred years and hopefully create a bridge between that world and this one. What I'm actually asking of you is to take part in a mission that once was like throwing a bottle into a small lake and hoping it gets to the other side and instead throwing it into an ocean and hoping it lands on a different continent." Dr. Rodriguez paused, the mood in the room was heavy, and somber.

Rick could see his crew trying to absorb the reality of their situation. He had sat in on other mission briefings in the past. While this one was a bit darker in tone than previous ones, the previous crews, he observed, always seemed less than excited to leave their lives on Earth.

"Alright, now that we have a sense of the big picture, let's bring it back to what we can appreciate, daily living. The next step is ship orientation and inspection, so I want Captain Lanson and his crew packed and ready for Space Station 27 in twenty-four hours. Assuming everything passes inspection, this will be where you spend the remainder of your time, so don't forget anything because there is no coming back. Everyone is dismissed." Dr Rodriguez gave a nod to the audience before walking away.

Rick worked to process the differences in the mission from what he had been expecting. He wasn't sure how much he cared about no longer being able to return to Earth. All of the concerns he previously had about learning 2,000 years of missed Earth history, a new language, a new culture, and whatever other things that much time might bring were all gone now. Jessica, who had sat next to him during the briefing, squeezed his hand and gave him a subtle nod as they made eye contact. Her gentle smile was all the reassurance he needed.

06 April 2336
Chapter 03

"So, Rick, what do you think? This is a pretty big deal. The first ship ever sent on a mission to find a new home for humanity," said Tim with a grin. He had a constant three day old scruff, short blond hair, and always wore tight shirts to accentuate the fact that he was the most muscular man on the crew. He served as both a structural and molecular engineer, though each person had been trained to perform most tasks the ship or crew may require.

"It's definitely exciting, but I'm trying to stay cool about it since it's going to be a long time before we get there, if we get there," said Rick as his crew reacted with disgust. They always gave him a hard time about never getting excited for anything. Rick looked around at the seven members of his crew. These were people that he had gone through all of his training with. He knew they were all as capable of being captains, like himself, and they were just as much his friends as they were his crew.

"I think I'm going to side with Rick on this one," said Taisha. She kept her black hair straight and cut in a short (in her words "efficient"), bob that bounced slightly as she talked. She often wore her crew jumpsuit. The blue accentuated her beautiful ebony skin, and conveyed an air of professionalism, even during down time. "It's all fun and games in the beginning, but when a few years go by with no reward, we'll start to lose sight of our goal if we allow ourselves to be swayed by our emotions. Especially since we aren't gone just a few years, but a few hundred years."

"Of course the psychologist would say that and ruin our fun. I mean, we are all painfully aware of the reality of the situation, as I'm sure I'm not the only one who got a letter this morning. But, I for one, am going to allow myself an extra amount of happiness to celebrate being part of a historical crew," said Matt, a handsome and boisterous Italian with a strong build, as he lifted his cup and everyone else followed suit. "Let us always remember that it is our love and happiness with each other that will get us through this journey. We live together."

"And we die together," the group responded in unison.

"Alright," said Taisha. "It is good for the health of the crew to get excited, sometimes you're right. If nothing else, I'll be glad to get away from those awful letters. No thank you for reminding me!"

The group sat quietly for a moment in Rick and Jessica's empty apartment. With the furniture returned to the positions they were in when Rick and Jessica had first moved in and the walls barren, Rick felt lost. He didn't live in this apartment anymore, and he had yet to see the ship he would soon call home. All he had to hold on to was the group he was sitting with currently.

...

"Alright guys, you know the drill. Drink the cup and take a run on the treadmill. Five minutes between each person." A young man dressed in a military uniform set eight cups on a table and walked over to his computer.

"I've heard the teleporters on the ship don't require a drink, and you keep your clothes on," said Jason. He picked up his cup and slowly twirled it to examine its contents. With a strong jaw line, a shaved head, black tattoos that peeked out from his mocha skin, and a constantly furrowed brow, Jason Taylor both looked like and acted the most seriously of the crew members.

"What's the point of the drink anyway? It's thick and tastes like charcoal," said Adelina as she choked down the sludge.

"It's just a safety precaution. Each drink has its own molecular ID which matches the shot we gave you an hour ago. When you first enter the transporter it scans you to take an image of how you are structured. The drink is thick and slow moving so that it coats you internally and helps get a cleaner scan. This is why you have to run for a few minutes, to speed up the process of it spreading throughout your body. Anyway, that scan information then gets associated with your ID and is compared to the final results after transfer to confirm success," said the young man as he typed away, preparing the machine for transportation.

He continued, "This machine has never had a bad delivery. We just do all of this stuff to be careful. Which is why we move clothing off of the body during transfer, so that there is no risk during the rebuild process. Your clothes get processed second, after the confirmed success of your arrival."

"So, Jason, you say they got rid of all this stuff for the teleporters on the ship?" Adelina asked as she jogged quickly on the treadmill. Her athletic, yet full, body easily endured the exertion as her long dark brown hair swished back and forth.

"That's what I heard, though I haven't seen it for myself," replied Jason.

"It's a shame if they fixed the clothes issue," quipped Matt as he walked over and gave Adelina a slap on the butt. He had black hair that he kept slicked back, and as the tallest member of the crew, he often wore shorts and short sleeved shirts to avoid the struggle of finding clothes that were long enough for him.

"My husband sure knows how to charm a woman. You know what works just as well at getting clothes off? Cleaning. You could also try making me dinner while you're at it," said Adelina with a grin. Her large brown eyes looked at him playfully. Her grin turned into a gorgeous smile, her red lipstick complemented by her olive skin.

"Alright, if you can please step into the transfer room, Mrs. Dawler, Dr. Rodriguez will be waiting when you arrive. You'll have two minutes to get dressed and clear the room before we begin the next transfer," said the man as he was typing. The door to the transfer room opened automatically and Adelina stepped in.

One by one the crew arrived and entered a room where Dr. Rodriguez, standing with a man decorated as a General, greeted them. A committee of five men and three women sat in chairs behind where the doctor and General stood. Each of them in their forties or fifties, wore lab coats, and carried an air of great importance. They sat across from another group of seats where the crew would be seated after their introduction.

"Doctor, you can take a seat and I will do the introductions, if you don't mind," said General Chen. He spoke with a commanding voice.

Dr. Rodriguez gave Rick a reassuring pat on his shoulder as he found a seat among the chairs, across from the committee.

The General shuffled reports in his hands to match the order of the crew that stood next to him. "First up is Dr. Adelina Dawler. She's twenty-three years old, majored in agricultural engineering and minored in nutrition. She wrote the paper *Engineering Food In Space*, which was used to drastically modify the design of the farm on the Titanic."

One of the men sitting down raised a hand and proceeded to talk without waiting for acknowledgment. "Dr. Dawler, can you explain how your research impacted construction on the Titanic?"

"It was a matter of refining the aquaponics process and understanding the impact of zero-gravity on fish," said Adelina.

"What exactly does that mean?" asked General Chen in a mildly frustrated tone.

"Aquaponics is basically a closed water system for plants that uses fish to provide the nutrients that plants need while the plants filter the water continually so the fish can survive. This is instead of soil-based farming which would require significantly more work to maintain healthy soil, and by that I mean it's basically impossible in space."

"Thank you," responded the General. His blank stare quickly revealed his lack of knowledge on the subject.

He continued. "Next up is Dr. Taisha Taylor, twenty-three years old. She majored in psychology and minored in art history. Her observation on relationships led to improvements in the Hype coupling program, which now has a success rate of ninety-five percent, versus the previous ninety-one percent. She also has done advanced research on the mental effects of isolation, which has improved the chance of mission success to seventy-three percent."

"Hmm, haven't we known for a while that isolation is bad? What did she find that improved our odds?" asked a stern female with her hair pulled tight into a pony tail, adding to the harsh expression on her face.

"I refined the crew schedule in a way that allows the right balance of personal space. The word isolation has a harsh connotation but is actually vital to the survival of an individual. Too much time alone can create paranoia and hallucinations, but not enough time alone can create group tension which could escalate into physical violence. People are more successful when they have time to be alone and organize their thoughts," replied Taisha.

"Well, improved chances of success are always appreciated. So good work," said the General. He gestured to the next person.

"Dr. Jason Taylor is twenty-three years old. He majored in mechanical engineering and minored in physics. He led the team that determined the most efficient angles for the ship's exterior in conjunction with the rotation and forward movement of the ship. Although it says here that his work only increased the speed by 0.05%, so I guess the ships initial design was pretty good before the team reviewed it."

Jason let out a disapproving snort. "Actually, 0.05% is a noteworthy improvement, which I guess is why it was in your notes," he retorted. "Point zero five percent of near light speed is about forty-eight million kilometers per hour. Over the span of three hundred years, that's nearly 144 trillion kilometers. That can be the difference in whether or not we live long enough to get there."

"My apologies," responded General Chen.

"Hon, you have got to relax. Not everyone is an engineer and can understand the significance of 0.05%." Taisha reached over and patted him on the leg to calm him. She was used to his reaction when someone seemed to underestimate his work. Hype worked exclusively with those who were advanced, but Jason stood out even among the gifted. While most people at Hype got their bachelor's degrees by sixteen, he had already written his thesis for his doctorate. Every crew member was required to have medical training, but Jason finished his training and was performing surgeries in half the usual time. It was therefore common for people to underestimate his accomplishments because of his age, and he didn't take it lightly.

"Moving on," announced General Chen. "Dr. Linda Bracy, twenty-two years old, she is the second agricultural engineer, and she minored in environmental studies. She helped develop the chemicals that will be used to condition the soil on the new planet to support the plants on the ship."

"Dr. Bracy, what do you think is the likelihood of the plants from the ship being able to survive on the new planet?" asked another of the seated men.

Linda, a tall and elegant blond with vibrant blue eyes, shoulder length hair, and a subtle tan, stepped forward slightly before speaking. "Considering this is supposed to be a planet capable of supporting human life with only minor conditioning, I would say it's pretty high. I have also designed several backup plans in case we have to adapt the plants to the new environment," responded Linda.

"Dr. Tim Bracy," continued the General. "At twenty-four, he is the oldest member of the crew. He majored in structural engineering and minored in molecular engineering. In his report it shows that he is the only one to have actually visited the Titanic during its construction, while the others reviewed documentation."

General Chen looked up from his notes. "So you've already had a chance to see the ship. What do you think?"

"I was glad the construction committee honored my petition, because I wanted to see first-hand the parts I would be maintaining. It's an amazing ship that has pushed the boundaries of technology and imagination. Very exciting," replied Tim.

"Then hopefully our tour of the ship will just be a review for you." Looking back at his notes, "Up next is Dr. Jessica Lanson. She's twenty-two years, majored in general medical practice, and minored in naturopathic medicine. She had a strong influence on plants that would be taken for medicinal purposes."

Jessica gave a polite nod to the committee.

"Dr. Lanson, do you feel the ship is properly equipped for any medical emergency you might encounter?" asked a woman.

"I've done my best to make sure that the ship is fully stocked with the plants we need to create most of the medicines we could use. We have the drugs and equipment necessary to perform basic surgeries and have implemented a strict diet and exercise regimen. Beyond that, everyone here understands the risk involved in this mission and there is not much more that we can do," answered Jessica.

"Dr. Matt is twenty-three years old, and majored in

medical nutrition with a minor in culinary arts. His report shows that he was four credits away from having a double major in structural engineering. How come you didn't finish?" asked the General.

"I just didn't feel the need to take some of the necessary classes. As a nutritionist and chef for such a small crew, I'm going to have a lot of spare time. I figured that I might as well learn enough to assist Tim with ship maintenance," replied Matt.

The General gave an approving nod. "Alright, the last one is Captain Rick Lanson. He's twenty-three. He double-majored in structural engineering and surgery. He earned the position as captain during general training, getting the highest average score across all areas of study." The General looked up from his notes. "Since I haven't been following this program from the beginning, can someone explain what exactly that means?"

Taisha spoke up. "After we graduated college we were given four years of general training. We were taught everything about running and maintaining both the ship and the crew. While each of us has our specialty, we are all technically capable of performing the duties of someone else, should the need arise. Captain Lanson's mind is uniquely broad in its ability to adapt to and understand a variety of situations and fields of study. While each of us here can out-perform him in our specific specialties, none of us have been able to adapt to the other crew members' roles as easily as he can. This makes him the most understanding of the needs of each crew member. As a result of that he has gained the respect of the crew and the position as our leader."

"Thank you for the explanation," replied General Chen.

"Good, now that everyone has been introduced, I can formally introduce myself and the people with me." He gestured for the crew to take their seats. "The people sitting across from you are a combination of Hype specialists and military mission strategists. I am General Chen and I have been in charge of the military's involvement with traveling to Planet D-173. While it is true that we allowed Hope In Extended Planetary Exploration to spearhead this project, the majority of the funding and manpower during construction was provided by the government. The tests each of you had to pass and the education you had to receive were all reviewed and modified by us. Each of you was picked not just because Hype approved of you but also because of your government's approval. However, you ultimately represent more than Hype or your government because the chance that either will be around by the time you get there is slim. This project has been the olive branch extended to other nations, and you can rest assured that whether or not it is us who makes contact with you upon your arrival, this technology and opportunity will be preserved and someone will be ready when you get there."

"That being said, we must still complete the final test of reviewing the ship. Assuming you pass, corrections will be made during the next two weeks, based upon your input, while you finish training and prepare for your departure."

06 April 2336
Chapter 04

Rick sat within the shuttle as it transported everyone from the space station to the Titanic. He could tell the shuttle was barely used and had a smell that reminded him of unboxing a new electronic device. He shifted in his seat uncomfortably. To say that he was nervous to finally see the ship he would spend the rest of his life on would be an understatement, and the hard plastic seat he was forced to sit on did nothing to help him relax. While he was able to see the ship from the station, as he approached in the shuttle, the size of the ship left him speechless.

The ship reminded him of a tuning fork. The majority of the ship consisted of two enormous prongs. The two prongs were joined together by tubes at one end, creating a U-shape that connected to a central shaft. From that junction of the two prongs, the central shaft extended forward into the cockpit, and the other end extended out of the back of the connection that led to the docking station. The ship was designed so that the two prongs could rotate around the central shaft to simulate gravity. There were two prongs because, if it were one long tube, it would be too close to the center of rotation and create disorientation. Because these two prongs had to be connected, they joined behind the cockpit, which did not rotate but stayed stationary as part of the central shaft. It was decided that weightlessness was easier to handle than the disorientation of being too close to the center of rotation. He had been told by those who had been on the ship that the worst part was going from the rotating tunnel to the weightless cockpit.

The shuttle traveled down the center of the ship to the docking bay. The size had been deceptive from a distance. Looking at the ship close-up made Rick think of two sky scrapers laying on their sides.

"We will start the tour in the docking bay and move to the cockpit. Due to the fact that the ship is still being worked on, there will not be gravity for the inspection. We wouldn't want to risk one of the arms knocking a guy out into space. They only make one and a half turns a minute, but it's better to play it safe," said General Chen.

The ship entered the docking bay, which seemed to Rick to be the size of a small house. The space easily contained the shuttle they arrived in and an additional shuttle. The room was also filled with equipment to maintain the ship.

"The docking bay is most likely the place you will spend the least amount of time. You can only use a maintenance shuttle when the ship is not running and because there is no gravity it makes work harder. Also, make sure you lock down the maintenance shuttles properly because you wouldn't want one floating around or it could crush you," said the General.

Red lights flashed as the hanger doors closed and the shuttle was parked and anchored to the ground. Rick peered through the window with anticipation. When the red lights stopped flashing and green lights blinked gently on a nearby wall to indicate that the room was now full of air, Rick exited the shuttle quickly, eager to tour the ship. He was greeted with the smell of fresh paint and electronics as he floated around and examined the room. Everything was attached to the ground securely, and all the drawers were latched closed. Rick opened a few drawers. They were all empty.

"Why are there so many drawers if they are all empty?" asked Rick.

"We designed the most complete facilities on this ship, more so than ever before. Previous missions were simply about surviving from point A to point B. However, this time around we want you to have the ability to create and adapt as situations arise, and we have provided you with tools and accessories accordingly. That being said, we slightly overestimated how much we could store in a zero-g area, so some things have been moved to storage areas or the maintenance warehouse. We have come up with some solutions, such as ties or lining the bottom of the drawers with magnets for anything metal. Those things have been ordered and will be installed in the next couple of days," replied the General. "Let's move to the cockpit so we can look over the interesting things."

The General led the way to the cockpit, followed by the crew, and trailed lastly by the committee members. The room was surprisingly simple. Rows of seats for crew members led the way to the control panels that lined the walls of the cockpit. Rick, having watched many old science fiction films in the past few years in anticipation of this trip, was surprised by how little detail the room had. The control panels were simple touch screens with digital dials and displays. The seats were a plain gray with five point harnesses, and the rest of the room was a clean white with no lines or distinguishing features.

"You'll notice the teleporter as you enter," said the

General as everyone floated in. "A month ago we were testing gravity and a couple guys wanted to see what the transition from gravity to zero-gs felt like. One of them described it by saying, 'Going from gravity to zero feels like jumping off a building, and going from zero to gravity is when you hit the ground.' He's obviously exaggerating, but just remember to keep your legs stiff so you don't fall over when gravity hits."

The General moved to the front of the cockpit. He floated before a giant blank wall that wrapped around half of the room. There were no windows inside the cockpit.

Linda looked around for a moment. "Okay, this may be obvious to everyone else, but I never looked over the blueprints for the cockpit, so I don't get it. Aren't there supposed to be windows so you can see where you are going?"

"Unfortunately, windows create structural weakness. While the ship's path is directed to avoid large objects and the exterior of the ship is designed to move small objects around the ship or absorb impacts through the shield, it's not a risk worth taking. Plus, there isn't much to see when traveling at light speed. If you want to see what is outside, you can hit this button." The General pressed a button on the console to his left, and the wall behind him turned black with small lights all over it. A man in a space suit flew by as the thrusters of his jet pack shot out small bursts of gas. "When the ship is at rest or at slow speeds, you can have a live feed of the view outside the ship. At light speed, the screen will show a single frame that can be refreshed as often as every 20 seconds. You can also view the sides or back of the ship. At light speed, all of these cameras will be taking pictures every 20 seconds. This data will be stored and sent to Earth anytime that you can connect with us. No point in wasting the chance to chart the deepest depths of space on your journey."

Rick examined the space closely. "It looks like things have moved around from where they were in the blueprints. You should be standing next to the emergency control board, General, but I don't see it."

"You are absolutely right. We ran through several emergency simulations and realized that most emergencies that needed immediate shut-down would occur when the cockpit was not in use. Therefore, it seemed like the best place for it was next to the teleporter so you could have instant access to it upon arrival."

Matt raised his hand slightly as he started to speak. "Wait a minute. Moving the 'emergency break' ten meters seems like a pretty insignificant change, unless you're implying that this is the only one. But why wouldn't there be one in every room? You know, in case of emergencies."

Adelina shook her head mildly. Rick knew that despite her outward display of disapproval of her husband's bluntness, she secretly admired his ability to confront an issue. He could see it in her eyes whenever she would tell a story about Matt's latest confrontation.

"Listen," said the General. "An emergency stop of the ship when it is at full speed is a serious issue. It takes several hours to bring the ship to a stop, not to mention the energy spent slowing it down or the risk to the crew from the force of the stop. It's not something we want you to take lightly by putting an 'emergency break' in every room."

Matt backed down quietly.

"You'll have much more time in here in the next two weeks during training, so let's move on," said the General as he led them out.

Leaving the cockpit, they moved toward a tunnel labeled "A". The tunnel curved slowly and came to an end at an open air lock.

"Every room can be sealed in case of an emergency. We also recommend that a room be sealed if there is maintenance being performed on the exterior of that section of the ship."

They moved down the large hallway. As Rick floated through the airlock, he paused in awe. From the tunnel, the space beyond the airlock seemed to explode into a six-story-tall space that extended for eighty meters before reaching a giant wall. The wall had a label painted on it large enough that Rick could read it from the other end of the space, 'Agricultural Environment Simulator,' and underneath that was painted 'A2' for the section of the ship.

On his left and right were rows of apartments. Each side had two rows of them, one stacked on the other, and five in each row, for a total of twenty apartments. Having spent most of his time looking at blueprints for home interiors, he had imagined them as townhouses and was disappointed by how little they looked like houses.

"This is where your homes are. They are pretty much just normal homes and I'm sure you've all seen the floor plans. Anything in there that might be considered mission-critical we will see elsewhere on the ship, so I'll let you guys explore them on your own time. If you're expecting a house warming gift from me, then I offer you a three trillion dollar space ship," quipped the General.

...

Rick pulled the hood of the wet suit over his head and shoved the hair sticking out underneath so it wasn't in his face.

"Normally you won't need a suit to enter the Agricultural Simulator, and you can keep the transition rooms at the entrances open, but when gravity is off, the water just floats in the air. Plants do fine in zero-gs, so there isn't an issue right now, which is convenient because turning the gravity off is the only way to get to the ceiling to replace a light bulb," said General Chen.

The room was over 200 meters long and was filled with all kinds of vegetation. Some areas were covered in crops that had just been planted and only stood thirty centimeters tall, while other areas had dense foliage that stood two to three stories high. The water floating around the crew bounced off their suits as they moved. The simulated sunlight cast hundreds of small rainbows around them that flickered wildly as the water moved.

Rick was surprised by how spotless the place looked despite all the dirt around the plants. He reached over and poked at the soil. "I thought we weren't using dirt," he said curiously. It squished under his finger, and water shot into the air. The spot expanded back to its original position as he removed his finger.

"It's high density foam. I'm not sure why they felt it necessary to make it look like dirt," said Adelina in response to Rick. "Linda and I came up with the foam as a solution to several problems. Each one has a specific density for the vegetation it supports. The machines that help maintain this facility can have a slightly more generic mixture to feed the plants and water the foam, knowing that it will only absorb the amount appropriate to the plant. This works as a sort of fail-safe to prevent errors from killing plants. This foam also holds the soil that the plant grows in, in place. This is why dirt isn't floating around right now with gravity turned off. The pressure from the foam on the dirt also helps secure the plant and strengthens the roots to promote growth."

"Yeah, but like I was saying, I thought we were using aquaponics," said Rick questioningly.

"We are, mostly, but that is primarily for the things we grow to eat, which require more water, and can be submerged in water. However, there are many plants here that require very little water, and in fact would die if overwatered. For those, we don't have to worry about maintaining their soil as much. Plus, we can still recycle the water they require through the aquaponics system to keep it healthy for the plants," replied Adelina.

"We've observed over the last three weeks that the machines do a great job of keeping the soil properly balanced and that they know how to harvest each plant. However, the one issue we have noticed so far is that the trimmers don't reach very low, out of safety to the people below, which means there is a lot that doesn't get trimmed. Luckily, two people spending a couple hours a day is more than enough to get the job done so it may just be a nice way to kill time," said the General.

The group moved through the vegetation. Most of the trees or bushes Rick had never heard of, but as they reached the transition room at the opposite end of the facility, he saw labels for corn, tomatoes, and rice. The group entered the transition room and the airlock closed behind them. A light overhead flashed red, and as they waited Rick could hear the sound of a vacuum turning on and he saw drops of water get sucked into grates built into the floor. When the air no longer had visible water in it, the light turned green and everyone began removing their wet suits.

Rick felt a sudden concern. "What do we do for food if the plants in there die?"

"Plant more seed," replied the General. "You have ten years of dehydrated food as a back-up which should give you plenty of time to fix any major problems. The machines can also detect dead plants and automatically remove them and reseed the area. Meaning, your only real concern is to properly maintain the machines. Do that and you'll be just fine." The General paused for a moment while everyone finished getting out of their wet suits. "Now, assuming we don't have any more questions, we can continue into the crew facilities," he said as he turned around and moved forward.

"The crew facilities contain both the mandatory and luxury items for maintaining individual health. Honestly, anyone can fix a machine, but to do that while also maintaining your physical, and mental health in outer space is almost impossible. However, with everything we have provided you with, you can be one step closer to success," said General Chen.

Rick entered a large area with tables and benches, couches, 2D and 3D televisions with connected devices for entertainment, and calming pictures on the walls. This seemed to be the only part of the ship that had any major decorations. Rather than the basic metal or white colors that everywhere else was swimming in, this place had warm earth tones and seemed inviting.

"The cafeteria and gym are here. The cafeteria will be automatically filled with fruit and vegetables that are harvested by the machines in the other room. If you want anything nicer than that, then you will have to talk to Dr. Dawler. Also, the machines will stock the items for you, but they won't throw them away if they go bad, so make sure to eat what's there or dispose of it properly," said the General.

The group paused in front of the gym. "The gym has been fully equipped with machines that will keep you fit, regardless of whether gravity is on or not. The gym is built to monitor the status of each individual while in use and can help select the appropriate video exercises when a user enters the video training area."

Tim examined the gym with excitement. He brandished his flexed bicep at Matt before giving it a kiss. Matt dismissed Tim's action with closed eyes and a shake of his head.

General Chen continued. "As far as the other luxury items go, nothing is complicated enough to waste time getting into it now. I will say, though, that my favorite part is the date area. It won't offer a ton of variety, but it's a nice little area with surround video that can give you a 360 view of the exterior of the ship or loop video of a few select places. If you can let your imagination go a little, then the beach setting could be nice." General Chen turned around and continued leading the group.

"Next is A4, the engineering facility," said the General as they approached the next massive wall with an airlock that was open.

The engineering room was nearly fifty meters long and the walls were lined with tools. The room was in stark contrast to the rest of the ship. While the rest of the ship contained at least the color of raw materials, the engineering facility was pure white. The rest of the ship used lights that simulated sun light, but this room had an almost sickening white glow.

"You are going to want to do as much work in here as possible, rather than in the docking bay. However, don't get lazy and leave things out. Should gravity go off while your tools are out or equipment is unsecured, someone could be killed by the loose items," said the General.

The crew moved through the space examining each tool casually. The large tools were strapped to the ground accompanied by equally large labels on the floor saying where each item went and how to properly secure it.

"We are now reaching the end of the 'A' arm of the ship. At the end of each arm is a mass accelerator and energy conversion unit. This stuff goes beyond my understanding, but, considering a few of you helped bring it to its current state, I don't think it needs an explanation," said the General.

The group passed through the air lock and stopped in front of the core, which was a twelve meter tall clear cube with tubes extending from it to the walls of the ship. Floating inside the cube was an eleven meter metal box, and at the base of every tube that extended out from the cube was a metal fan. Rick was surprised by how simple such a complex machine looked, but he knew that all the interesting things were inside the giant metal box. In front of the clear cube was a control panel, which Rick knew was primarily for emergencies.

"Because the core is the life of the ship, it is important that each of you be trained on the basic functions and maintenance of the unit. Dr. Taylor will prepare you all to handle most emergencies that might arise in the next two weeks." The General moved in the direction of a nearby teleporter. "We will now jump over to the storage room near the end of the 'B' wing. There is an identical core at the end of the 'B' wing, but the teleporters do not allow anyone to teleport into a core room, only out. This is a safety feature so that no one jumps into a dangerous situation unknowingly. In an emergency involving the core, it is likely that the teleporters will be disabled completely. They take up significant power that could drain your backup power quickly, and you also wouldn't want the power to cut out mid jump."

...

Rick moved out of the teleporter and saw a red light turn green, signifying that the teleporter was clear for use. He was surprised by how natural it felt when it didn't require a bunch of rituals to use. Rick found himself surrounded by shelves. Twenty-four rows, two stories high, and forty meters long, he couldn't imagine how he would find anything.

"Don't worry," said the General, acknowledging the overwhelmed look on Rick's face. "The entire system is automated. Just punch in the item you want at the terminal and it will be retrieved for you. If you aren't sure what the name of the item you are looking for is, then you can search for it by category. Bear in mind, everything for ship, core, or shuttle maintenance is in engineering. If you need to clean something, fix a toilet or whatever, that's in maintenance. Storage contains everything else, like food and toilet paper. Now if you don't mind, I would like to move to the lab."

The group moved through the aisles in the storage room, Adeline running her fingers across the shelves as she moved, and reached the opened airlock leading to the lab. The lab had the same bright white light that the engineering room had. However, the lab was more inviting because of the earth-tone colors used on the walls and carpet.

"Anything that you want to see with a microscope or have computer-analyzed happens here. We spared no expense getting the most powerful software available, and while the lab will mostly be used for medical purposes, we also acquired the most accurate organic matter analysis software out there. Assessing the proper treatment in the garden can now be done with extreme precision. The system will notify you when anything more than minor changes are required. Manual reviews can also be done by you to check the accuracy of the system," replied the General.

"Interesting," said Tim as he reflected on his observations. "It just started to make sense to me that the ship is not laid out in a very logical way, unless you expected us to travel by teleporters more often than not. It seemed weird, though I let it go, that the crew quarters were separated from the crew facilities by the garden. But what really threw me off was that the next room was not the medical area. The lab, which you said will be mostly used by us for medical purposes is separated from the medical bay by the maintenance facility."

"The ship is laid out starting from the cockpit and moving back by importance for survival, from the most basic needs back to mission-critical or replacement items. We started with the crew quarters and medical in 'A1' and 'B1', respectively. The next most important things beyond immediate survival are long term survival and repairing the facilities. 'A2' is the garden, and 'B2' is maintenance, which is not where you would typically do ship repairs. However, engineering had to be next to the engines, so maintenance was the next best option. The crew facilities, 'A3', and the lab, 'B3', are almost entirely expendable. For a long term mission they are critical to success because they address deeper health and happiness issues, but in an emergency they are completely extra. The same could also be said of the refinery upstairs because it creates medicines and conditions the air through purifiers and such, but survival at its basic definition is possible without it. Finally, everything from engineering and storage could be moved to other areas if required," replied the General.

"Now, if there are no objections, I would like to skip the refinery for now, since it is just a bunch of automated machines that you won't see unless something breaks. We can also breeze through the maintenance room since it is a simplified version of the engineering room," said the General.

General Chen continued to move. They passed through the maintenance room that had significantly more spare parts in it than engineering, but less of the heavy machinery. They continued, arriving at the airlock leading to the medical facilities.

As the group began moving through the medical facility, Rick thought it seemed more like an office building than any doctor's office he had visited before. With no lobby, receptionist, or posters pushing medicines at him, he felt as though he would come here to get his taxes done rather than get a physical. Rick glanced through a window to a room and immediately recognized surgery equipment. "I thought the operating room was supposed to be on the second floor?" He asked.

"The original layout accommodated the most commonly used rooms first. While we expect most surgeries to be planned and most injuries to be mild enough to allow an additional minute of travel to the second floor, we decided it wasn't worth the risk that something could happen where someone was close to death and survival would be decided by a minute. You may lose time going to the second floor for every appointment, but it's worth the chance that this could save a life," replied the General.

"I would think it wouldn't matter because of the teleporters," said Taisha.

"That was the thought process for the original design of the ship's layout. Unfortunately, the teleporters only support one person at a time. If you have someone who breaks their leg and needs to be carried, there is no way for everyone to get through a teleporter without having to drop the injured individual. Plus, stretchers would never fit through a teleporter," said the General.

General Chen moved into an operating room as the group followed behind him. "You've got a tough situation here. The people putting themselves at risk of injury are the same people who would perform surgery if someone were injured. I would recommend that, whenever possible, leave your best surgeon behind. Let's not fail to recognize the fact that every time you exit the ship you are entering an environment that could kill you. So leave your best medic on the ship when you can." The General moved toward a large body scanner. "We've provided you with the best tools out there and we will make sure you know how to use them within the next two weeks."

General Chen gestured to the exit. "Now, if you all will please make your way through the airlock, we can return to the docking bay."

. . .

General Chen followed behind the crew as they made their way back to the docking bay. "Captain Lanson, why don't you hold back for a second so I can talk with you."

As the crew moved into the docking bay Rick stayed in the tunnel to talk. The committee members, who had previously lingered behind the crew and the General, moved up beside Rick. The General looked in the direction of the crew.

"Any concerns about the ship?" asked the General.

"Things seem to have moved around a little from the blueprints I last saw, but it seemed to be out of necessity. I feel comfortable with what I saw and your answers to my questions," replied Rick.

"How do you feel about your crew? Anyone you have issues with or would like to change?" asked a female committee member. This was the first time Rick had noticed any of them say anything since arriving on the ship.

"No, I've spent the last four years with most of them. They each have their flaws, but they are my family. We need each other if this mission is going to be successful."

"You've shown that you are observant with your questions. You are a leader among your peers, and you allow them to speak freely, yet they treat you with respect," said a male committee member.

"I have confidence that you are the right choice for the mission," replied another.

"Do you believe you and your crew can be ready in two weeks?" asked a different female.

"I have no reason to believe otherwise."

15 April 2336
Chapter 05

Jessica set two drinks down on the table and dropped into the seat across from Rick. She wore a knee-length green dress that she knew was Rick's favorite. It complemented her fiery red hair. They had been working fourteen hour days for the past week, and today was the first day they had since arriving at Space Station 27 to relax.

S.S.27 had two restaurants on it that were constantly full. With the mission less than a week away, the station was at full capacity. Nearly 1000 people were on the space station working around the clock. With rotating schedules to minimize down time and personnel overlap, there were always over 100 people to fill each restaurant. One restaurant was formal while the other was a casual bar and grill. People rarely ate the free food in the cafeteria because the restaurants reminded the workers of home.

Rick sat silently for a moment soaking up the atmosphere that he knew he would only experience a few more times in his life. The music played just loud enough that he had to raise his voice to talk, and the air had a weight to it that could only come from being in close proximity to a large number of people. The crew planned on meeting around six, but Rick decided to take Jessica early so they could spend sometime alone.

"Everything seems to be happening so quickly now that we are here," said Jessica.

"It's definitely a bit overwhelming," replied Rick.

Jessica reached over with delicate and slender fingers and grabbed Rick's hand, giving it a reassuring squeeze. "At least we have each other to get through this." Her hair glowed in the soft light of the restaurant. Her alluring green eyes sparkled as the candle on the table flicked in the air, and Rick's heart melted as she gave him a loving smile.

"You've always made me feel like I could do anything. I'm glad we had this time together. I always feel renewed when we get to be alone," said Rick.

Jessica leaned over and kissed his cheek. "I don't think finding time to be alone will be an issue once we leave here."

. . .

Everyone arrived at the restaurant promptly at six. The time off was greatly appreciated and no one wanted to be late. Everyone quickly took seats. Before anyone started talking Matt stood up, the dark light of the restaurant accentuating his tanned skin and making his hair look jet black.

"This is the first time we've been able to enjoy ourselves since arriving at S.S.27," began Matt, "but the crew and I thought something had gone without celebration for far too long and now was the best time to correct that."

Jessica produced a small box from her purse and handed it to Matt.

Matt continued. "Within any group of friends, there is always that one person that serves as the core, the heart of the group, without which the group would lose much of what makes it unique and special. Rick, you are, in fact, statistically the right choice as a leader, with the best understanding of the broadest scope of knowledge. But you are also the heart, not just of the crew, but of our group as friends. We don't follow you because of how smart you are, but because we love you, because you draw the best out of us."

"I came into the mix later," interrupted Jessica, "as did Adelina and Linda, through the partnering program. However, we could immediately see why the men of your crew, and Taisha, were so fiercely loyal to you. Everyone feels like they have a place in the group. No one feels bossed around or bullied. You hear us out on everything and make decisions that take everyone's different needs and opinions into consideration."

The rest of the group nodded in agreement.

Taisha stood. This was one of the few times she did not wear her standard uniform. She wore a form-fitting romper that showed off her slim and graceful form. "You all know I love my man. Being the only couple here that came together by choice rather than through the partnering program, I had the luxury of seeing what I was getting myself into. This crew, these friends, and your leadership, Rick, made the decision a thousand times easier. There could have been no other captain among us."

Matt cleared his throat. He held out the box Jessica had handed him and gave it a slight jiggle. "You lovely ladies are stealing the spotlight that was clearly supposed to be on me."

Everyone laughed.

"Anyway, to officially celebrate your confirmation as our captain, we all decided to give you a gift." Matt handed Rick the box.

Inside the box Rick found a gold watch with a white face with black numbers and gold hands that clicked slowly with the time. "Wow," he uttered in a whisper.

"We know you love antiques," said Tim. "No hologram display, no bio-sensors, no email, heck, it doesn't even have a digital display. It is from the late nineteen hundreds, when a watch could only tell the time."

"I love it," responded Rick as he promptly put it on.

"We have complete faith in you to lead this mission successfully," assured Jason.

With the surprise ceremony out of the way, talk among the crew remained light. No one desired to discuss the mission or that this would be one of the last times they would enjoy a public place. Shadow Space Colony would be their only other chance, but that wouldn't be for a long time. They also knew that enough time would pass that when they finally reached Shadow Space Colony they may not be able to cope with large groups of people. Rick knew this was likely the last time they would enjoy a public place, even if they experienced one again.

The group sat quietly drinking their beverages and picking at the appetizers Jessica had ordered before they arrived. Rick continually stole glances at his watch, elated by the surprising, and thoughtful gift.

"Hey Rick," said Matt, finally breaking the silence, as he gave a wide grin. "Did you ever tell Jessica how you tried to cheat your way out of the partnering program?"

"Excuse me?" exclaimed Jessica. "This better be a good story, or we are going to be in for a long 270 years," she said as she cracked a faint smile.

"Thanks Matt, like any good friend, you're always

looking out for me," said Rick.

"Stop stalling and tell the story," said Matt.

Rick let out a long sigh. "Alright. So a couple weeks before we were going to find out who the partnering program had picked for us Matt comes up to me and says he got a peek at who I was going to be partnered with and that it was someone I had never met. He assured me that the logic behind the pick was solid. It's done with computers, after all, and that he had met this girl before and she was perfect for me. Of course, I immediately get concerned that I have never met this girl and if Matt thinks she's cool then there must be something wrong with her."

"Naturally," pipes in Matt.

"So I decided that I was going to prove the program wrong and pick someone for myself since they would give preferential treatment to your current partner if you already had one. There was this girl, Brea Johnson, that I had a crush on, so I told her she should come to my place and I would make her dinner. Now, I should preface this by saying that at the time I had no idea that Matt apparently went out of his way to agitate Brea whenever he was around her."

"You never noticed, but she was very uptight and it was very easy to upset her," added Matt.

Rick responded with a disappointed nod of agreement. "Anyway, I was almost entirely done making this stew that just needed to simmer for a while longer, which I had timed to be done right after I picked her up and brought her to my place. Before I left to go get her, the guys were hanging out with me in my apartment and they were right in the middle of a level in this game when I needed to leave, so they promised to leave and lock up before I got back. Also, Matt had snagged my phone when I wasn't looking so I couldn't find it when I needed to go and I was forced to leave without it.

"Of course, going and getting her was no big deal. We're getting along fine and she seems plenty excited to be coming over, so I'm feeling confident. Then we arrive at my apartment and the nightmare begins.

"The place was locked up and nothing was obvious when we first stepped in. As far as I could tell, everyone had left and everything was fine. We walk in and I tell her she can take a seat on the couch while I go check on the food to make sure it is done. You can't imagine how dumbfounded I was when I looked into the kitchen and the place was immaculate. I'm not just saying my dirty dishes were clean. I mean, the place was empty. I'm not even sure how they did it. My soup was gone and there wasn't a single dirty dish or utensil left out. I looked in the fridge and there weren't even the remains of the ingredients I had used. You would never be able to tell, other than a slight lingering smell, that I had been cooking in there."

"We just stole the soup and utensils and replaced them with our own," clarified Tim. "The soup was good, by the way."

"However, before I had a chance to fully process the first disaster, I heard Brea from the other room let out an awful groan before making a sound like she was trying not to throw up. I run to see what's wrong and I notice what has to be the most obviously used pair of underwear ever sticking halfway out from between the seat cushion and arm rest. I mean, it was somewhere between a wet fart and full-on diarrhea."

"Which is all the more impressive," interjected Matt, "because they were fully submerged when I had placed them there, which meant she had to really give them a tug to do that kind of investigation."

"Yes, and by the way she was holding her hand away from herself, she clearly didn't make a completely clean investigation. Immediately I declared my innocence, but she just looked at me with disgust and asked for the bathroom. I point her toward it while I start making my way to the kitchen to grab a bag to throw the underwear into but make it half way when I hear her scream. So I turned around and ran to see what had happened this time and unfortunately got there soon enough to see exactly what had scared her, though I wish I hadn't. Matt is crouched on the toilet with his butt in the air pointed toward the door, and his pants and underwear are at his ankles. Though if you are imagining a typical mooning, you are wildly off base.

"First off, Matt is a very hairy person. So imagine a carpet of hair. I don't know if I should say it extends up from his legs or down from his back. Either way it's impressive. Secondly, again, don't think of this as a typical mooning because Matt was also using his hands to fully spread his cheeks and since he was also bending over, literally everything was on display. It's probably the thing I most regret seeing in my life. Though it was followed by one of the best things I ever saw.

"When the shock wore off and she remembered why she had run to the bathroom, which was to wash her hand, she stepped in and shoved Matt away from her. He screamed as he toppled over, with zero control since his hands were behind him and his ankles were basically tied together with his underwear, into the bathtub and got a pretty good-sized, and fully justified, welt on his head."

"I won't say I didn't deserve it," acknowledged Matt.

"She is now shaking with rage and tears are starting to well in her eyes, and she looks at me and asks, 'Is this vulgar animal part of your crew?' Which I had no option but to mournfully nod yes to. Then, to top it all off, as the three of us are standing outside the bathroom, while she is absolutely reaming Matt, my phone starts ringing over my Bluetooth speaker."

Rick shakes his head and shrugs.

"I never set that up, but it got all of our attention and somehow the call goes through, though I never answered it, and for some reason I was unable to respond. Anyway, they got some girl I don't even know to call and she says, 'Hey Rick, not sure if you can hear me. I know you've been having phone issues, but I wanted to say sorry I ran out on you last night. I was just caught off guard by the whole thing. I mean, I've never been asked to do something like that. It was definitely weird, but the more I thought about it, the more I figured I should just give it a try. I mean, we still do that other thing that was a bit scary at first, but now I'm cool with it. Anyway, call me back when you aren't having phone issues and we can have some fun. Bye!'

"At this point Brea has just had enough and I've given up all hope of trying to salvage anything. She winds up with a slap that I knew was coming and just accepted my fate. After that she stormed out and all Matt could say before I forced him to clean up my couch was, 'She's not the one, dude.'

"Obviously, a couple weeks later I found out they were completely right and had saved me from making a big mistake." Rick reached over and put his hand on Jessica's leg. Looking into her eyes, he said, "I felt more for you from the first second I saw you than I ever felt for her. I never could have picked someone as great as you."

Jessica leaned over and gave Rick a kiss. "Thanks boys, I can't believe that for once you guys actually *prevented* my husband from being an idiot. Though, I am a little surprised that someone as by-the-books as you would have tried something rebellious," she said to Rick.

"I was always okay with leaving into space and traveling my entire life into the unknown. Accomplishing a mission for the sake of others, it was all very factual, something I didn't need to question. It had purpose and value, so I was cool with it. However, being told who I would do that all with, who would keep me company, who would make me happy, and love me, that seemed hard to leave in their hands. Who were they to tell me what was in my heart? Obviously, I was wrong to doubt them, since they knew better than I."

The crew stayed in the crowded restaurant and continued to tell stories for several hours. Rick knew that everyone, like himself, wanted to savor their last moments before embarking on a trip that they could not return from.

23 April 2336
Chapter 06

"Ladies and Gentlemen, today's the day," said General Chen. The General paced slowly in front of the crew that was gathered in the docking bay of Space Station 27. "We have spent the past two weeks making sure that you are all familiar with the ship and how to properly maintain it. Our goal was that each of you could be replaced by at least one other member of the crew, should the need ever arise. Captain Lanson has reviewed the progress each of you has made and believes that all of you are ready for this mission.

There will be open communication for the next four days until your ship reaches a speed that hinders communication. You will have a three week period when you do your scheduled maintenance in two years when we will be able to communicate with you again. That will be twenty years from now for me, if I can join the conversation I will. If I can't, your next stop won't be for another twenty years for me. I plan on being retired or dead in the next forty years, so this is likely the last time I will talk to you. It's been a pleasure working with each of you and I have full confidence in this crew to be successful. Good luck on your journey, guys."

"Some pep talk," whispered Jason to Rick. "Remind the crew that everyone they know will be dead in four to six years, right before they leave. I'm glad we won't be getting any more motivational speeches from him."

The General stood next to the steps leading into the shuttle and shook the hand of each crew member as they entered. Tim sat in the pilot's seat and prepared the shuttle while the others found places in the passenger seats. The door closed as the General stood, giving a final salute.

Rick's stomach knotted in anticipation. He wasn't too concerned about what he was leaving behind since he was going on the trip with all the people he cared about most. Though his mind was flooded with thoughts about the journey and everything that could happen.

When the door was fully closed a chime rang, signaling a successful air-tight seal. The intercom clicked on as Tim spoke. "Let me just get this moving, then Rick can give his orders."

The rotation of the docking bay slowly stopped and the shuttle gently lifted off the ground. Tim fired the thrusters and the shuttle moved forward toward the airlock. They came to a stop in front of a large door which opened immediately after the one behind them closed. The intercom clicked on. "We just cleared the doors and will arrive at the ship in a couple of minutes. Rick, if you want to get started, it should be smooth sailing," said Tim.

"Honey," said Linda. "We can hear you just fine, you don't need to use the intercom."

The intercom clicked on. "As long as it's here, I'm gonna use it." Tim said with a grin as he set down the microphone.

Rick got out of his seat and moved to the front of the shuttle. "It's finally here. Years of training and preparation have led us to this point." He looked out the window at the approaching ship. The arms rotated slowly for the simulated gravity. The size of the ship never stopped shocking him.

"But let's not lose focus here. We are nothing compared to the value of the mission, and the mission has little chance of success. I'm not trying to bring anyone down. My point here is that there is no need to get excited and make quick decisions. We are going to take this slow and do it right. Let's let Earth screw this up, not us."

"When we get on the ship I want everyone to be in the cockpit and ready for launch in fifteen minutes. That will be enough time to make sure everything is secure and ready. And remember, this is what we trained for. This is our purpose and we've got this in the bag," said Rick as he gave a nod to his crew.

Rick sat down among his crew and stared at the arms of the ship that now rotated around him as the shuttle neared the docking bay. The ship was coated in a white, semi-reflective material that helped deflect heat generated by nearby stars and planets. It now reflected the shuttle clearly. Through the window he could also see a faint reflection of himself, and he got a brief glimpse of the concern that painted his face. He quickly forced a smile and pushed himself to convey confidence.

The shuttle passed through the first of the two doors. After the first closed, a green light flashed and the second door opened. The shuttle moved gracefully into the docking bay toward two clamps in the ground that were open. As the shuttle descended upon the clamps, they closed around the hook bars on the bottom of the shuttle, securing it in place. As the door to the shuttle opened and his crew prepared to leave, Rick looked at the faces of his friends and noticed a change. The calm, lighthearted expressions they had, just moments ago, were now replaced with seriousness and purpose.

"You know your job, now get it done. You've got fifteen," said Rick firmly.

"Yes, Captain," replied the group in unison.

As each person left they went directly to the teleporter, stopping just long enough to punch in the code of where they needed to go. Rick knew that a thorough sweep had been done an hour ago by the maintenance crew, but Rick would never pilot a ship that his crew hadn't inspected personally. He didn't expect to find anything, which is why he only gave them fifteen minutes, just long enough to do a quick sweep to find anything obvious.

Rick moved out of the shuttle. Only Tim remained in the docking bay as he inspected the shuttles and surrounding equipment. Most of the past two weeks had been spent on this ship, yet Rick had not spent much time in the docking bay. He moved to the drawers that he had opened during the inspection. They were now filled with tools, all held in place by magnetic plates attached to the bottom of the drawers.

He continued through the docking bay and into the passageway leading to the cockpit. Glancing at his watch, he noticed that eleven minutes had already passed. As he entered the cockpit he noticed the red hair of his wife.

"That was quick," said Rick. "And I notice you took the time to secure all the beautiful."

"All the beautiful what? Oh, you mean, I contain all of the beauty of this ship, and therefore it is secure... with me." Her voice adjusted to sound formal. "Excuse me, Captain Lanson, now is not the time for such poorly executed pick-up lines," said Jessica with a smile.

"I apologize, Mrs Lanson. I guess I will have to wait until

tonight to be distracted by how gorgeous you look," said Rick as he moved to the front of the cockpit, giving Jessica a kiss on her forehead as he passed her.

One by one the crew teleported into the cockpit. Rick enjoyed watching their faces as the shock of teleporting into weightlessness hit them. Rick looked at his watch as the last crew member arrived with ten seconds to spare. The crew looked sharp and ready as they sat buckled in their seats.

"Did anyone find anything out of place?" asked Rick.

The crew sat silently, waiting.

"Jason, were all the gauges reading properly on the mass accelerators?"

"Yes, Captain," his dark brown eyes, and steely gaze emanating determination.

"Adelina, after basic inspection, the vegetation looked to be healthy?"

"Yes, and I also quickly skimmed over a printout of the last three days of computer scans and everything looks good, Captain." Her olive skin still glistened from the humidity of the Agricultural Environment Simulator.

"Alright, crew. Are we ready?"

"Yes, Captain," replied the crew in one voice.

With that, Rick moved to the control panel and typed in a pass code above the button labeled 'Initiate Launch Sequence'. Upon pressing the button, a screen on the wall in front of him came to life. The message on it read, "Is the crew secure?" with 'yes' and 'no' buttons below it. Rick touched the 'yes' button. The message changed, "Engine room clear and ready for launch initiation?" Rick glanced at Jason, who gave him a quick nod. Rick pressed the 'yes' button on the screen. The screen then read, "Launch sequence initiated."

27 April 2336
Chapter 07

Jason sat, staring intently at the screen in front of him. "The ship has just reached full speed," said Jason. "And all the gauges are showing perfect numbers."

The last two weeks had been spent watching gauges obsessively. Jason would fine tune things when a gauge would get a little high or low, but Rick was surprised by how uneventful the two weeks were. He quietly watched the stars on the screen in front of him change as the picture was refreshed while he sat in the cockpit. He leaned forward and pressed a button on the console near him, and a green circle with a microphone appeared on the screen above. The intercom was on.

"I'd like to get everyone together in the cafeteria in five minutes," said Rick. He turned off the intercom and pushed away from the console. He allowed himself to float out of the cockpit and into the tunnel. He preferred the smooth transition into gravity rather than teleporting into it. He often chose walking over teleporting because it made him feel less lethargic yet forced him to keep a slower pace.

As Rick walked through the crew quarters, he noticed how the crew had already changed the feel of the ship from when they had first arrived. Slowly, the sterile white exterior of the crew quarters morphed into inviting homes. Other than getting the ship up to speed, the crew had spent the last two weeks settling in.

Matt had always wanted to own a house but decided the closest he would get to that was to put a doormat in front of his door. It read, "If you lived here, you'd be home by now." His goal, he said, was to have the highest valued property on the ship. No one bothers to remind him that the apartments have identical layouts, or that there are sixteen unoccupied apartments. *Supply and demand are not in his favor*, Rick thought to himself.

Taisha had chosen to decorate her front door by hanging a painting she had made next to it. Everyone was so impressed with her painting of a sunset on a beach that she had several requests from the other women for artwork that could go in their homes.

Rick reached the door to the Agricultural Environment Simulator, what the crew now called the "Agrosim," and chose to use the teleporter for the rest of the distance. The Agrosim was humid enough that, even a short walk through it, made him sweat horribly. It was the one area he consistently skipped.

Rick waited for everyone to take a seat before speaking. "It's been roughly two weeks since we left. We just reached full speed and from here on out, to keep things simple, we will only refer to local time rather than Earth's time. Otherwise we are going to be celebrating a lot of birthdays over the next 3,000 Earth years and it will be confusing as far as what age the girls should start lying about how old they are." He looked around at the faces of his crew. Everyone seemed to be in a somber mood.

"How is everyone adjusting? Does anyone have anything that needs to be addressed?" asked Rick.

"The evaluations so far seem to be normal," answered

Taisha. "Everyone is going through the standard amount of mourning and mild depression. However, we all seem to be turning the corner into acceptance, as expected, so I have no concerns. This will of course come in waves as traumatic experiences often resurface three to six months later, as well as annually if we don't create enough positive associated memories. However, everyone thus far seems to be applying the techniques learned in their pre-trauma counseling appropriately, so I am hopeful that long term issues will be minimal if not entirely avoided."

"Glad to hear that. I want you to keep a close eye on that over the next two days." Rick paused and looked at the group. "Two days, guys. That is how long you have to make sure you have everything together before we have our first run in the sleep chambers. We will be in the sleep chambers for two months so don't leave any food or drinks out because they won't smell good when you wake up.

"When the two months are up we will do full examinations, both physical and mental, to make sure the sleep chambers are working properly and that our bodies are coping. A full psych exam will be performed. We've all heard about extended sleep producing strange dreams and that the dreamer can have a hard time separating them from reality. The plan then will be to get some exercise and check the ship and then back to sleep. We will sleep for four months at a time after that. We will wake up, repeat the previous procedures, exams and all, and then back to sleep again and again until it's time to wake up and slow the ship down for a full test and analysis of ship performance and safety. Any questions?" asked Rick.

Adelina raised her hand slowly and Rick nodded to her in

recognition. "How long are we going to be awake in between sleep cycles?"

"For now it will be two weeks awake each time. I know it sounds a little off, but the sleep chambers are safest and most successful the healthier, and therefore, younger you are. We have a lot of ground to cover and it's best to start early. The older we get, the more time we will spend out of the sleep chambers."

Rick paused for a moment. It was easy to get overwhelmed when talking about the big picture. "Alright, enough with everything that is *going* to happen. Something that *has* happened is we reached full speed successfully and without issue. We have taken our first huge step with a level of success to be proud of." Rick gave the crew a moment to rejoice. "Now make sure everything you have left to do is done within two days. Everyone is dismissed."

The crew separated slowly, with each of them leaving in groups of two or three. Rick sat in the cafeteria watching and listening as everyone started their own conversations about the ship as they left. At any given moment he knew he could find at least two people talking about one of three different things: the ship, what they thought was happening on Earth, and what they thought the new planet would be like. He wondered how long it would take for those conversations to become mundane. He guessed that discussions of Earth would be the last to go. There are only so many theories and guesses one could make about the new planet based on the evidence that had been provided, the ship would eventually stop being fascinating and become just another house chore, but Earth was the one thing that had the outside influence of other people. Wondering what technology would evolve into, what wars were being fought, other planets found and their resources gathered, or if humanity had simply died out were all questions that would remain and would continue to be relevant to their work. Thus, that was the one conversation that might never go away.

Soon everyone had left and Rick was reminded of one of the many oddities he had never experienced before being on the ship, pure silence. It had not occurred to him just how much of the outside world had bled into his every waking moment until it was gone. No sound of weather, traffic, talking, or yelling from the thousands of people that always surrounded him. Nothing. Be it man-made or nature, something was always making noise, but not now. There were places one could go to be surrounded by the whirring of machines, or to simulate the sounds of nature, but the majority of the ship could be purely silent if he let it. It was the kind of silence that revealed any minor imperfection in his hearing, that amplified the squeaking of his joints when he moved, or made him feel as though the air had taken on a mass that could crush him. A silence that became painful if he focused on it, a mental struggle he could never win.

He hoped he could eventually adjust to his new environment and learn to not just expect it but embrace it. For now, however, he knew it was best to get up and get busy.

11 May 2336
Chapter 08

A gentle breeze blew against Rick's face and arms. The strong smell of water and salt engulfed him. He opened his eyes and was met with a blinding light. Slowly his vision adjusted to reveal an ocean sprawling out endlessly before him. Warm sand fell over his toes as it gave way under his weight. He looked down and saw he was wearing white clothes that hung loosely on him, allowing the soft wind to reach his skin. He felt at peace.

He looked to his right and saw a beach that extended beyond where he could see. Behind him was a tropical jungle with dense foliage that created a green wall pushed up against the sand. He looked to his left and saw the same limitless beach that was on his right. A small yellow dot could be seen between the white sand and blue sky. Rick squinted as he walked toward the yellow form as it slowly took shape, and he saw Jessica coming toward him.

Rick began to jog toward her, his strong build moving effortlessly, and she matched his pace. Her yellow dress clung to her elegant form, revealing her feminine curves, as she gracefully moved over the sand. Her movement seemed effortless as she joyfully came to him. Her long hair blowing behind her in the wind. When they finally reached each other, she jumped into his arms and embraced him tightly.

"I've been waiting for you for quite a while," said Jessica as she looked at Rick with a slight pout. "You didn't even get any firewood like you said you were going to. What were you doing this whole time?" Jessica paused, but cut Rick off as he started to reply. "You can be so easily distracted sometimes," she said as she leaned in and kissed his cheek.

Her skin was soft, porcelain white, and had a sweet smell to it.

She smiled at him thoughtfully and squeezed his hand. "It's okay. I gathered some wood for our fire while I waited for you. Let's get back to our picnic. I'm getting hungry."

Birds chirped quietly from the trees as they walked along the beach. Jessica drew herself close to Rick, wrapping her arms around him as they walked. Her body was close enough that even with their movement as they walked he could feel the rise and fall of her chest as she breathed.

"It's nice that we finally get to go to the beach together," she said.

"It is what you always wanted for a honeymoon," responded Rick.

"Too bad we were never able to go on one since Hype wouldn't give us the time off."

That comment stung Rick mildly. They walked quietly for a moment. He had never liked how Hype had taken away the grand spectacle of a young relationship. There was no story about him asking her out for the first time or how he proposed. They didn't have a large wedding or a honeymoon. He didn't care about those things for himself, but wished he could have had a chance to show Jessica how much he loved her through those events. At least, he thought, they would always be able to laugh about their first date.

"This is so much nicer than a sim room could ever

create." Said Rick with a smile.

Jessica peeked up at him and returned his smile. "It really is wonderful, especially since your friends can't replace the video projections with a horror film," she said with a chuckle. "You sure were nervous for the rest of that date."

"Yeah, well, they kind of ruined our first date. I didn't know how you would react," responded Rick.

"Tim told me later that he knew I was the right one because I was unfazed by your friends. It was just a perfect indication of what I was always going to be in for." She squeezed him tighter.

They walked quietly for a moment, still embracing each other. Rick enjoyed the gentle crash of the waves and the sound of the water rushing up the sand and hitting their feet. He loved the warmth of Jessica's soft body pressed against his.

"While you were gone I found this great place just inside the jungle. I moved our picnic there. You've got to see it," said Jessica as she gave a tug on Rick's hand.

She then let go and moved quickly through the sand toward the dense trees. The trees seemed to swallow her completely as she entered. It was impossible to see her from where Rick stood.

Rick paused for a moment, completely caught off guard by the sudden change. He quickly ran in the sand to try to catch up to Jessica. As he reached the wall of trees, he immediately felt overwhelmed by how thick the jungle was. He struggled desperately to follow her as branches scraped at his face. In the distance he would get brief glimpses of her, quick flashes of red amid the trees, as she moved gracefully through the foliage at a speed that shocked him.

He was fifteen meters in and had lost sight of Jessica. He looked behind him and saw that the beach was no longer visible. Rick quickly became disoriented. He continued to move forward, unsure of the direction he was now moving. The moist smell of the jungle overpowered him as feelings of claustrophobia began to take hold of him. He tried desperately to listen for Jessica, to find her direction. He began yelling, but the trees seemed to absorb the sound as it left his mouth.

As he struggled through the trees, vines, and bushes, he heard a loud crack overhead. The birds in the trees exploded into a flurry of panic as they escaped the branches into the open sky. Rick could hear a loud commotion moving toward him quickly, but he could not see anything as he strained to peer through the branches. Suddenly a dark object could be seen falling above him, but he was unable to move through the forest that had engulfed him until it finally struck him on the head and threw him to the ground. Rick's world became black.

11 July 2336
Chapter 09

Rick woke up exhausted, his exasperated breathing leaving a white cloud on the clear lid above him. He looked to his left to see Jessica in her sleep chamber as she slowly opened her eyes. She smiled the same loving smile at him that she always did.

"How did you sleep?" asked Jessica, her voice muffled by the sleep chamber.

"Well... I'm glad to be awake." He let out a big yawn and struggled to stretch within the confines of his chamber. "How about you?"

Jessica attempted to rub the tiredness from her eyes. "We had dinner and went dancing. If this is what sleeping for months at a time is like, then I'm not sure I want to wake up. I could never get you to dance with me."

He gave her a doubtful look. "How was I?"

"You were awful. I loved it." Jessica stretched out and winced. "How do you feel? Any joint pain or stiffness?"

"No, but the muscles in my legs feel a little weak."

"Yeah, same here. We'll have to up the strength on the electric pulse muscle stimulation next time. I just didn't want to start off too strong."

The lid to Rick's sleep chamber opened automatically after the oxygen balance became equal to that outside the chamber. He sat up and began removing the straps to the muscle stimulators. He slowly walked over to the intercom, his limbs tingling as though they had just finished being asleep.

"Good morning everyone. Hope you all slept well. I want everyone to get a status update and report to me within two hours. Jessica will make the rounds while you work to do a brief physical exam. Psych exams will be performed later unless anyone feels they need one now. I'll see you all soon."

Jessica walked up to Rick from behind and gently kissed his back. "As long as I have to make the rounds, I might as well start with you," she said as she gently rested her stethoscope on his back.

"Deep breaths." She slid the stethoscope on his back after each breath. "Does everything feel okay? Any tightness?"

"No, I feel fine," replied Rick.

"Alright, take a seat and tell me if anything I do hurts."

Jessica started by bending his arms and legs to test the joints. She then began massaging different muscles. Rick winced when she rubbed his calves.

"The muscle feels like it should and I've already seen you walk, so I'm betting it's just a little sore. I'm sure it will pass quickly. Now stand up so I can check your back."

Rick stood up. She rubbed the muscles in his lower back, her slender fingers caressing his sides as she worked. She gently kissed the side of his neck.

"That's not how you give everyone's exams, is it?" asked Rick.

"I find it helps my patients relax," she said with a slight grin. "Everything looks good. Now go be the Captain I'm proud to be married to."

. . .

The crew sat in the cafeteria eating breakfast after doing their rounds on the ship. Rick had not been hungry when he first woke up, which was common, but hunger hit him quickly, and hard as he had been reviewing the ship's status.

"I've reviewed the logs of the core and everything seems to be fluctuating within normal levels," said Jason. "There were a couple peaks in core temperature, but they were likely from solar waves or some other external variable. However, the systems responded appropriately every time and temporarily slowed core speeds long enough to bring the temperature down. This of course, would have occurred in a matter of seconds, so we never would have known."

"That's good to hear," responded Rick. "How are our plants doing?" He asked as he turned to Linda.

Her blond hair was lazily tied up behind her head as she ate. "Everything appears to be doing well. The plants and soil seem to have maintained the perfect balance of chemicals. The only issue I noticed was that the trimmers hadn't trimmed quite enough. It's nothing alarming, but it does mean extra work after a long sleeping period if we can't iron it out," replied Linda.

"Jason, I want you to help her figure out how to lower the trimmers to handle more of the work. I know it was made in a specific way for safety, but let's get the machines working the way we want and we can just learn to be safe around them," said Rick.

"Yes, sir," responded Jason.

Rick turned to Tim. "How's the ship looking?"

"System scans and external pictures look good," answered Tim. He leaned back in his chair casually, which bulged his chest through his tight shirt. "There's only so much I can tell you until we can get out there and actually take a look at things. I'm not concerned about anything, but I won't feel confident until I get some hands on time. Unfortunately, that won't be for months."

"I guess we'll have to trust the system to recognize changes in the hull's appearance. I know the software is under tested, but it's our only option right now," said Rick.

Tim shrugged. "Yeah, it's almost worthless at this point because it throws up warning messages over everything, even chipping paint. Granted, those were mostly at the beginning of our trip, and the software is slowly learning what is an acceptable range of hull shifting. But it's a hell of a time sifting through the warnings for any actual data."

"I know this seems almost unnecessary right now because the ship is new and the data is limited, but let's not get lazy after a few uneventful ship reviews. There will be a time when an analysis like this will save our lives, so let's stay sharp," warned Rick.

Rick raked his fingers through his hair as he turned back to the group. "I'm proud of everyone here. We all made it this far for a reason, and we are going to succeed at our mission for that same reason. Now is the time when we start developing a rhythm to everything we do, so let's make sure that quality is a part of that rhythm. I think we are done here, for now, as long as no one has any major concerns to address. Taisha is going to call each of you in for a psych review after this meeting, so don't get involved in anything you can't stop. You're all dismissed."

. . .

Rick sat quietly in the hallway outside the counseling office, his brown hair dangling in his eyes as he examined the floor between his feet. Built into the wall at the end of the hall was a window frame. Inside the frame was a screen playing a looping video of an outdoor area. There was nothing exciting about the video, just the exterior of a random building in front of a street. No cars or pedestrians ever went by, so the loop was not obvious. Sun emulating light bulbs were used behind the video to produce light that splashed into the hallway and created a comforting warmth. His apartment had similar windows in certain rooms, but he had grown to dislike them as he felt it created a false sense of hope that he would ever truly leave the ship.

After several minutes of waiting, the door to the office opened. Jessica popped her head out. "You can come in now."

The office seemed large because of the limited furnishings. There was a small desk with a computer on it and three chairs. The walls were a comfortable light brown and were bare except for a whiteboard on one wall that had abstract shapes and limited words on it. Their meaning was lost to Rick.

He sat in the last of three seats, across from Jessica and Taisha, who seemed in good spirits. Rick was happy to match their attitude. "How's my crew doing?" asked Rick.

Jessica crossed her long legs as she scanned her notes. "My observations show that everyone is physically healthy. Several people had muscle soreness like you had, and Tim had some minor breathing troubles, but all symptoms passed by the time I did a check up on him an hour later. I've made all the necessary changes to everyone's sleep chambers which should prevent these issues in the future."

"That's good to hear. Taisha, how did everyone sleep?"

Taisha sat proudly, continuing the professionalism she was known for when work needed to be done. "Everyone is textbook so far. Everyone had positive dreams that were generally calm. There are several factors that come into play here, of course. The higher oxygen levels in the sleep chambers create a natural euphoric state. Everyone was generally excited about using the sleep chambers for the first time, yet ultimately calm because of the state everyone was in as far as coping with the isolation of the trip. You, Rick, are the only one to have any negative moments in your dreams. However, a feeling of loneliness and being lost are not things I'm concerned about. There is significantly less data on captain sleep habits than for the crew and your added responsibility would imply the extra chance of a stressful dream. This does not contradict what little data I have."

Rick was relieved to hear such a positive review of his dream. He knew stress could make for bad dreams, which is why he hadn't explained every detail of his dream. He told Taisha he had woken up as something was about to hit him from above. He knew that the truth, however, was that he had been killed in his dream by that falling object, though he had always read that you can't dream of your own death because it's not something you've ever seen or experienced before. However, he assumed stress could make you dream things that were not always steeped in reality.

Rick let out a sigh of relief. "As long as no one has any major concerns then we will maintain our current procedures and schedule."

15 March 2338

Chapter 10

"Begin the deceleration process." Rick's voice was filled with excitement.

"Yes, captain," replied Jason. He proceeded to press a button on the control panel and several warning and confirmation boxes appeared on the screen in front of him. He addressed each message and then declared, "Deceleration process initiated."

A siren gave a short blast over the intercom, followed by a female voice that announced to the ship, "Deceleration process has successfully begun. Estimated time of completion is six weeks, one day, seven hours, and twenty-seven minutes."

"How do you feel? Any concerns?" asked Rick, feeling mildly anxious.

Jason turned from the control panel and looked at Rick. His face showed signs of concern. His dark eyes were intense. "Exiting the light wave and switching the mass accelerators to standard propulsion is always dangerous. Without the light wave to act as a shield, moving things in front of and around us, we are at risk. The ship's computers have detected a couple airflow anomalies, likely a mild bowing of exterior plates due to heat, that need to be addressed. However, I believe the integrity of the hull is solid and trustworthy. We should be fine."

...

"I wish I wasn't going to have to trim these branches for the rest of my life," said Linda as she hacked away at a thick branch. Sweat dripped down her face as she worked. Her hair sweeping her shoulders with each aggressive movement. "It's amazing how much they grow while we sleep."

"Didn't Jason help you fix that a while ago?" asked Rick.

"He looked at it with me, but it's not a matter of it functioning properly. The machinery is attached to the ceiling and wasn't built to reach low enough to get to the bottom branches. It's short by about one and a half meters."

"Well, Tim's the structural engineer. I'll have him help you figure it out. Is everything else going alright?"

"Yeah, the crops are growing well and the food is being properly stocked in the cafeteria by the machines. Nothing to report," she said with a grunt as she continued cutting branches.

"Glad to hear that," said Rick. He turned away from Linda, careful not to walk into any branches, and followed the path to the crew facilities.

...

"I've gone over the numbers several times and I believe we can adjust the plates to deflect solar waves better on the last panels of the inner channels, which would protect the core more and increase efficiency," said Jason.

Jason sat at a table with papers covered in numbers and diagrams sprawled out in front of him. Rick and Tim sat across from him as he presented his information.

Tim looked over the notes. Despite freshly shaving after emerging from the sleep chamber, he was back to his constant three day scruff. "You might be right, but it seems risky to be making adjustments at this point, the stakes are high."

"We still have five weeks left before we come to a stop," replied Jason. "That's plenty of time to run the numbers and get a game plan together for executing this quickly and safely."

"How quickly do you think we can make the changes you're asking for?" asked Rick. "I don't want the engines to get cold, or to run on reserve power for too long."

"You can install a normal exterior plate with only three people. A shield plate is a little harder and would take four. If we tackle them at the same time in two groups, it shouldn't add much time at all. I also figure we could program the computer for the new hull shape before we come to a stop. It would pump out errors until we make the changes, but it would also let us know quickly if the installation was successful. The engines would still be warm when it's time to fire them up again," said Jason.

"I thought the channels were perfectly uniform. How is there any way that you could improve things?" Rick asked doubtfully.

"The ship's plates actually have very gradual bowing to them that is unique to each panel to help funnel heat and radiation into specific patterns around the ship. At the beginning and end of each funnel are our shield plates. The first one obviously takes the brunt of the force as it begins the funnel and the end plate curves out slightly to launch the heat and radiation away. There are two specific funnels, one on each arm of the ship, that I think I could improve," replied Jason excitedly.

"Alright, you two have four weeks to make this happen with a week of testing and preparation for installation. If we come to a stop and your idea isn't fully proven, it's a no-go," responded Rick. "Tim, I also want you to help Linda fix the vegetation trimmer. We hit the sleep chambers shortly after the relaunch, so you will have to work on these projects at the same time."

"Yes, sir," replied Tim.

...

Steam rose into the air. Rick blew on his coffee as he waited for it to cool. Over time he had forgotten what coffee from fresh beans tasted like. The pouches used to preserve the coffee beans worked well enough and he no longer could tell the difference. He yawned hard and took a sip from his cup.

With only two days left before the ship stopped, the crew had spent the last six weeks preparing for the maintenance they would perform. The vegetation trimmer had been fixed, Jason's heat panels fabricated, and a clear plan devised for maintenance execution. With all tasks completed early, the crew felt the need to celebrate. They sat around a table in the cafeteria, talking loudly.

"Most of my chamber dreams are pretty boring, running late to class or being unprepared for a test. That sort of stuff. My favorite dream I've had a couple times is that I'm flying around on a giant sponge. I can go wherever I want and see everything," said Adelina.

"Wait, did you just say a sponge?" asked Tim.

"Yeah, a giant one."

"Like... the kind you find in the ocean?" asked Taisha.

"No, a square one you clean dishes with." Adelina threw her long dark hair behind her shoulders and crossed her arms, pretending to get defensive.

"Why in the world would you dream about a sponge? You don't even do the dishes. I do!" Exclaimed Matt, who then laughed loudly.

"Laugh all you want, but when I'm with my sponge I can go wherever I want and see anything." Adelina acted indifferent to the group's laughter before finally cracking a smile. "How 'bout you Rick? What have your sleep chamber dreams been like?"

Rick took a sip of his coffee and shrugged. "Nothing exciting." He knew they could see the tension underneath his calm facade.

"You've at least had a few good ones, right?" asked Jason. He put a large muscular arm around Rick's shoulder.

"Well, when I'm lucky, I just don't dream at all," replied Rick.

"Oh, come on!" exclaimed Jason. "You always dream. You just don't always remember it. But we all know that's not true for sleep chambers. The dreams occur so slowly that you don't forget it."

"Sometimes I'm asleep and I only see black. I realize that I'm asleep, so I just wait it out," replied Rick. He gave another shrug.

"We are only two years into this journey and you're already being a downer. You better lighten up or you're gonna die before all of us," said Jason as he gave Rick a pat on the back.

"We all know that captains have a history of less enjoyable dreams. As long as he's not dreaming about killing the crew, then he's doing alright to me," said Taisha.

Everyone gave an uncomfortable chuckle.

"Geez, honey! You have never been able to make a good joke!" exclaimed Jason.

25 April 2338
Chapter 11

Jason and Tim sat hunched over their keyboards as text scrolled quickly on the screens around them. Thirty-eight hours earlier, the ship started receiving data packets. Jason knew this would happen and was actually surprised that it had taken so long to start receiving them.

"I shouldn't have gone back to sleep!" Jason said to himself angrily.

"No way you could have known the packets were encrypted," said Tim as he sat back in his chair.

"The ship sends a direct signal to Earth when it's going slower than light speed, right?" asked Rick.

"It doesn't open a direct connection because the computational power required to interpret quantum connections would use too much energy. Instead, when we dip under light speed, the computer sends a blast of data packets with all relevant information to Earth," replied Jason.

"Then how do they talk to us if we don't keep the connection open?" asked Rick.

"There's two steps to the process. The first step is that once the ship is going slow enough to receive messages, our quantum connection sends quick pulses to Earth simply to signal that we are available and then turns off. They then trigger our computers to turn on when they are ready to transmit with timed pulses of sent information. Obviously, if the computer is not on then it can't read a message telling it to turn on, so a sensor, which takes almost no power, listens to the quantum connection for basic pulses. The right combination of pulses and the computer turns on," responded Jason.

"Information cannot be stolen or scraped from a quantum connection, so why are the messages encrypted?" asked Rick.

"The notification of a received message that our ship gives me is the same regardless of the source. The messages we started receiving, which I just assumed were from Hype, weren't quantum. They were radio. They are encrypted because they could be scraped. If only I had known they were encrypted back when we received them, we would have all the messages by now. There was also a bit of wasted time because I didn't realize they were bloating the message."

"What does that mean?" asked Rick.

"That means that only one out of every twenty data packets received is relevant. It doesn't actually prevent stolen data. It just slows the thief down. If you think that all twenty pieces of information are important, then you are going to waste time trying to translate nineteen worthless pieces. You will also spend time trying to fit those nineteen translated pieces into a message that they aren't meant for. Eventually you would figure it out, but the hope is that the person the message was actually intended for would figure it out first."

"Wait," said Rick with a confused look on his face. "We have been traveling at the speed of light. How could we be receiving a radio message?"

Jason rolled his eyes. "I can't get into the specifics about it right now, since it isn't important. But, a long long time ago, in a galaxy far, far away, we observed pulsars, which are rapidly rotating neutron stars. These stars sent out radio waves in pulses, with greater strength, that traveled farther distances, than we thought possible at the time. Long story short, we learned how to do that."

"Sorry for asking. So we are receiving a random, encrypted message? What have you found out so far?"

"The first message basically explained that these messages were automated. It goes on to briefly mention some civil unrest and that all missions are to continue as planned and that any messages stating otherwise should be ignored. It also said that their level of communication, or lack thereof, moving forward should not be viewed as a form of mission failure. Communication may be silenced as safety precautions," said Jason.

Tim shook his head. "It's being sent over radio waves, which means it's a mass communication message. Apparently they didn't bother programming an auto-response with the quantum connection and they felt the need to encrypt the message. That's all a bit unsettling."

"Honestly, I'm not too surprised," replied Rick. "There were a lot of politicians lobbying for some radical ideas on how to prepare for future droughts and limited resources. Remember the comment Dr. Rodriguez made, accusations about this mission being a political stunt? I wouldn't have expected such severe reactions so soon in the opposite direction, but it was going to happen eventually."

"Yeah, it's a little odd that we could get messages telling us to go back, but what is most interesting is that the filler content they put in to bloat the message is all news articles," said Jason as he scanned through the headlines. "I don't think wars will start up over limited resources for at least fifty years, our time. There has been talk of rationing supplies for ages, but these articles seem to be about pollution and the general living quality of a lot of people. Government-funded companies around the world started making some really bad decisions, and it looks like several nations have had coups in an attempt to band together and eliminate the corporations that were ruining poorer area living environments. Looks like a lot of people were getting paid under the table and a lot of those people are now dead. I sure wouldn't want to be on Earth right now."

"So it sounds like they might try to call us back to take our ship for resources," said Rick, frowning.

"If so, then they would be too short-sighted to understand that we are trying to help Earth in the long run," said Tim.

27 April 2338

Chapter 12

Matt swore to himself silently.

Preliminary diagnostics showed that shuttle two had an electrical problem and wouldn't start. It had been determined that it would take less time to move the exterior panels for the ship to the other shuttle than to try and fix the electrical problem. Matt, Adelina, and Linda had spent the past hour trying to fit all the panels into one shuttle.

"The storage space wasn't made to hold this many panels. It's going to be a tight fit to make this work," said Matt.

"Luckily we have enough anchors to unload all the panels for team one and don't need to go back and forth to drop off panels. That's going to save a ton of time," said Linda.

Matt finished moving the final panel into the shuttle, his substantial form moving gracefully in zero gravity, and closed the doors to the storage area. "All done," he said triumphantly.

"Just in time because the ship should be at a stop soon," said Adelina.

As she spoke, the remaining crew members entered the docking bay, followed by Rick.

"Is the shuttle ready?" asked Rick.

"Yes, sir. All the panels have been placed in shuttle one," responded Matt.

"Good. I want the engines to be as warm as possible when we fire them back up, so let's make this quick. Just remember, quality matters most, so take the time you need to do the job right, but nothing more," said Rick.

"Yes, sir," responded the crew in unison.

"Alright, Tim and Jason, take charge of your teams and get this done. The ship will be stopped by the time you are ready in the shuttle. I will monitor your progress from the cockpit," said Rick.

"Let's buckle in and get this show on the road," said Tim.

The crew began entering the shuttle and taking seats. Tim made his way to the driver's seat.

"We'll stop and drop off the exterior panels first and then move to the other section of the ship to replace the shield panels. There are fewer exterior panels to replace, but they take longer to install. We should be able to knock out our four panels before you finish your three," said Tim to Jason.

"Sounds like a plan," replied Jason.

Tim began to turn on the shuttle. The shuttle lurched forward as the engine came to life. He then released the locking mechanism and the shuttle floated up effortlessly.

...

Rick watched from the cockpit as the shuttle arrived at its first stop and the crew began removing the exterior panels. It took nearly ten minutes to remove each panel and anchor them to the ship. The anchors were long enough that the panel could be maneuvered into place without worrying about them floating away. As the crew began moving the first panel into place, the other two floated peacefully.

"Careful with that shuttle. I don't want to get burned up!" Exclaimed Matt, his concern masked with a joking tone.

"Yeah, yeah. Just stay out of my way," replied Tim playfully.

Rick listened to their conversation over the radio as he watched them on his screen.

Tim fired his side thrusters to turn the shuttle so that he could fire the rear exhaust away from the four crew members outside of the shuttle. Rick could tell that the shuttle was difficult to steer. Tim was close to the panels and fired his side thrusters to try and avoid them. As Rick watched, a panel shot forward.

"Watch it!" yelled Jason.

"You shouldn't have pinned me in!" Snapped Tim as he gunned it before the panel had a chance to block him again.

Rick quickly leaned in toward the monitor he was watching to examine the shuttle. A white mist floated near the impact point. "Status report now! What's that white stuff coming off the shuttle?" questioned Rick.

Jason moved to the panel that had been hit and examined it. "Everything looks fine. Luckily, these things are really strong. From here it looks like the white particles from the shuttle are paint chips. No noticeable damage that I can see."

Rick let out a deep sigh of relief. "Okay, we got lucky. Let's stay focused and get this job done." He was suddenly very anxious, having his entire crew outside of the ship.

Tim flew the ship to its next destination and the crew began removing the first panel. Yellow caution lights on the screen in front of Rick turned to red as the two teams removed the original panels. When Tim's team had finished replacing their first panel, a red light turned green. Rick looked to see Jason's team as they were finishing their first panel as well.

"The computer says we are green for the first shield panel. Looks like you nailed it with the fabrication," said Rick.

"We have good tools, so I was never too concerned, but it is a relief," replied Jason.

One by one the yellow lights in front of Rick turned red and then green. The work didn't appear too difficult as Rick watched his crew, though it felt incredibly slow as they floated around outside.

Finally, Tim, Linda, and Jessica began returning to the other team just as the last exterior panel finished installation and the control panel gave a green light.

"All panels have been successfully installed. Let's bring it in so we can fire this ship back up," said Rick, not bothering to hide his excitement at bringing everyone back inside.

"Jason, when we get back to the ship we are going to have to take a look at the shuttle. The panel must have done more damage than we can see because the left side jets don't seem to be firing very well and acceleration is slow," said Tim.

"Sounds like maybe a fuel line is pinched, probably nothing major. You're almost here. I'll take a quick look before I get on board," replied Jason.

"Tell me if you see the left jets firing in a second, when I turn," said Tim.

The radio was quiet for a few seconds as Rick watched the shuttle on his monitor.

"See anything?" asked Tim.

"No, and it doesn't look like you are turning. See anything different from your angle, Rick?" asked Jason.

"Just a little flicker from your thrusters. If it is a pinched fuel line than maybe you just have to give it a bit more gas," replied Rick.

"Let's see what happens," said Tim.

Rick watched the screen, waiting to see what would happen. The thrusters lit up more than the previous attempt and then quickly went dark.

"What happened? It felt like it was working and then cut out," said Tim.

Looking closely, Rick noticed mist coming from the dent in the shuttle.

"I'll try giving it more..."

"No!" screamed Rick. "Cut the engines!"

A quick flash of orange shot out, licking up the gas that had escaped. Just as quickly as it had shot out it was sucked back in and a small explosion instantly threw the shuttle into a spin toward the crew outside. Rick could hear Jessica and Linda screaming over the radio.

"Rick!" pleaded Jessica, her voice fraught with terror.

Matt was shouting at Adelina to get out of the way as he attempted to push her before the shuttle hit them both. The shuttle was moving too quickly to escape, but before it hit them a second explosion ripped the shuttle in half. Rick could see it had killed Matt and Adelina instantly as their bodies remained lifeless as they were thrown from the shuttle.

Tim, who had been closest to the second explosion, flew out in multiple pieces, his blood crystallizing as it hit space.

Linda's mask had been fractured and Rick saw her grasping desperately at the cracks in her mask, her legs kicking wildly in panic for a moment until she finally went limp.

Jason and Taisha had been thrown by the explosion of the shuttle into the ship. Rick could see gas escaping from a canister on Taisha's hip that he knew was oxygen. She began searching for more oxygen, but the bodies she could reach were too destroyed and the shuttle had moved too far away for her to reach it. Jason had hit the ship on his back, which made the jet pack on his back explode. The explosion threw him into space, unable to slow his speed and return to the ship. His arms waived frantically as he hopelessly reached for the ship that moved farther and farther away from him.

As Rick watched in shock, he saw Jessica float out of the shuttle. Her body was lifeless. Rick watched desperately, hoping for any form of movement, but there was none. He stared at the screen, helplessly, unable to think or move. He knew there was nothing he could do since the second shuttle was in need of repair and had not been fully diagnosed yet.

Seeing Jessica float away, completely motionless, left Rick in shock. He shut down entirely, his body refusing to process what had just happened.

Taisha had given up hope of finding more oxygen and curled up into a ball. "I love you, Jason. I'll be okay, sweetie," she whispered to Jason.

Rick finally turned away several minutes later after she stopped convulsing as she died.

Jason could no longer be seen trying to repair his jet pack so he could return to the ship. For several minutes he had been repeating over his headset, "I can fix this. Taisha, I can fix this. I'm coming back to you." Rick had been too stunned to interject before Jason was too far away for the radio to work. His words slowly crackled more and more until they

they faded into silence. The suits had up to four hours of oxygen in them. It would be a while before he died.

29 April 2338

Chapter 13

"What is your mission status?"

It took a moment for Rick to register the noise he heard. The sound jolted him awake from the mental fog his shock had placed him in.

"Please respond and report on the status of your mission," said a young-sounding male.

Rick squinted his eyes in an attempt to steady his vision. His hand shook furiously as he reached for the button to respond. He had not slept more than a couple of hours in the last two days. His stomach felt like it was filled with a thousand needles when he moved. He had only left the cockpit long enough to go to the bathroom and drink water.

"Is anyone there? Please respond."

"This is Captain Lanson," said Rick with a voice that struggled to escape his dry and hoarse throat.

"Our logs show that your ship has been stationary for the past fifty-three hours. What is the status of your mission?"

Rick tried desperately to overcome his exhaustion. "Mission status is ... uh."

"What is the status of your ship?" interrupted the man over the radio. "Is it still functional?"

Rick looked at the panel in front of him. Colored lights indicated the ships status. Hull integrity: green, surface integrity: green. The panels had been installed properly and the ship had not taken damage from the explosions of the shuttle. He fought hard to push the recent events out of his mind and focus on what was happening now. He scooped his sweaty and matted hair away from his face in an attempt to compose himself. "The ship is fine."

"Good, good. Listen, Hype has retracted all missions and is bringing all the ships home. If your ship is functional, then we need you to come back as quickly as possible."

"For what purpose?" asked Rick, finally gaining awareness.

"Many people have lost their homes to pollution. Your ship could offer a clean, sustainable living environment for significantly more people than are currently using it. We will also send it to much closer planets to gather resources."

Rick thought he could almost hear the contempt in the young man's voice. He slowly took control of himself with this distraction, his voice more steady. "This mission is to save future generations, isn't abandoning the mission being short-sighted?"

"The mission is a pipe dream!" snapped the young man. "The problems aren't a thousand years in the future. They are now! We need that ship."

Rick stopped and thought for a moment. He didn't want to keep resources from those in need, but the success of the mission could save millions of lives. However, the chance of success was nearly, if not entirely, impossible now. Could he survive the mission alone? He knew that if anyone found out what had happened they would cancel the mission, but then the deaths of his crew would be meaningless.

That final thought pushed him over the edge. His crew, his wife, his friends, had died while repairing the ship. They had spent half of their lives preparing for this mission, and now this man wants to bring the ship back, to turn it into a living complex, and to dangerously mine nearby planets. It would be a ridiculously small band aid on a global problem that would do a complete disservice to what the ship and it's crew stood for, and Rick would not allow this.

"Listen, I would love to keep talking about this, but I'm falling behind schedule. My orders are to complete the mission at all costs. I have strict instructions to not return home. Good bye." Rick pressed the button to end communication before the man had a chance to respond.

Rick instantly felt heavy and exhausted. He initiated the launch sequence for the ship and made his way to his home. Every step he took and every movement of his arms threw shooting pain through his body. His exhaustion was so strong he nearly collapsed several times as his head would dip forward while his body fought his will and attempted to force him into slumber. He didn't know what he was going to do, but he knew he needed sleep, so he climbed into bed and slept.

...

Rick ate slowly. He had waited long enough to eat that he no longer felt hunger. His stomach hurt furiously, but he could hardly keep his food down. Since he had woken up he had felt at peace. He knew that the initial shock had worn off and that he was currently in denial of what had happened. He took advantage of his ability to function and nourished himself.

He decided that the easiest thing to do was to stay focused on his tasks. He was planning to use the sleep chamber when the ship reached full speed, and would use it for six months rather than four. He would have to be extra thorough with his preparations so that everything would still be in control when he woke up.

He stuffed his pockets full of fruit and whatever snacks he could find. He needed to bring his weight up from what he had lost over the past few days if he wanted to survive the sleep chamber, but he couldn't bear to be still. The first time he tried to eat at a table he became so overwhelmed, and cried so strongly, that he decided the best thing to do was to stay busy, even when eating. He also chose to work until he could no longer keep his eyes open because he otherwise would lay in bed for hours, never able to stop thinking long enough to sleep.

Occasionally he wouldn't stay awake long enough to make it to bed and would wake up in the middle of the task he had been performing. He was always careful to choose small tasks when he started getting tired so that he would not get hurt if he fell asleep.

He now made his way to the Agrosim to do some pruning. It was too exhausting over an extended period of time in his current condition, so he chose to do it gradually, a small amount each day. He began to sweat almost immediately after entering the Agrosim. The temperature was kept ten degrees warmer and the added humidity made the room feel heavy. Soft shadows lay still on the ground, and the simulated sunlight hit his face randomly as he walked through the tall vegetation. The only movement or sound was from the automated arms above the plants. A slight hum could be heard as some machinery trimmed branches and other machinery swept over flowers gently to pollinate them.

Rick picked up the pruning sheers and began trimming the low branches around him. Linda had left the tools out since she had intended to return to her work after the panels had been installed. Rick had easily found them and resumed her work.

Early on he had taken the time to clean up everyone's mess throughout the ship. After getting his hopes up several times when seeing someones tools or dirty dishes out, he knew it would be easiest on himself to put everything away. It broke his heart to clean everyone's things, to acknowledge that they were never coming back, but he knew it had to be done and would hurt less in the long run.

After an hour of gardening, Rick had worked up a sweat and decided to go to the docking bay to fix the remaining shuttle. He was heavily winded and chose to take the teleporter rather than walk.

...

Rick floated outside the teleporter, staring at the docking bay. It felt empty with only the one shuttle. Rick had not entered the docking bay since the accident, until today. There were articles of clothing inside the crew lockers that they had changed out of to get inside their suits before they had left. Rick felt more alone in the docking bay than anywhere else on the ship because of how empty it was.

The diagnostic tools and Tim's notes lay on a work bench near the shuttle, held in place by the magnetic surface. Several panels on the side of the shuttle were open, exposing wires and circuit boards. Rick looked at Tim's notes, which were a list of different circuits and connections he had tested. At the bottom of the list was "diode 81" and "transistor 17," both with question marks next to them.

Rick skimmed through the shuttle's schematics until he found the locations of the two items. Picking up the diagnostic tools, he bent over and began examining the circuit boards. As he counted up the numbers in search of transistor 17, he became aware of how quiet the docking bay was. He looked around the docking bay and saw only a sterile, white, empty room. He shivered slightly as a tingle went down his spine.

Rick turned back to the shuttle to resume his work as he suddenly felt a hand lay gently on his shoulder and then grip tightly. Rick froze in fear. An alarm began ringing, signaling that the bay doors were about to open. Rick attempted to turn around and stand, but the hand on his shoulder gripped harder and pushed down so that he could not move. A second alarm went off, followed by flashing red lights throughout the bay. The exterior bay door was about to open while the safety interior door was still open. The sirens rang for several seconds before Rick saw the door begin to open.

As the door first began to separate Rick's ears were filled with the screaming sound of the air being pulled into outer space. The bay quickly fell silent as the gap widened. As the air moved to the opening faster, he could feel his clothes begin to pull on him, though the hand that gripped him held him firmly in place.

Rick's lungs began to burn as he tried desperately to breathe. His eyes became dry, but as his eyes watered the tears were pulled from his face before providing relief. As the air left, the coldness of space engulfed him, making his skin feel like it was filled with needles.

Overwhelmed by pain, he had forgotten about the hand that had pinned him down until it finally let go. Nearly all the wind had died out as the docking bay approached equilibrium with the outside, leaving just enough to slowly lift Rick up and send him drifting out of the bay doors.

Rick could no longer breathe. He tried to reach out to grab for anything nearby, but his movement was restricted. He struggled to look down at his arms and saw that they were covered in blue ice. His blood was being pulled through his skin, but freezing to him before it could float away. His vision turned red, from the blood that filled his eyes, and then began to narrow.

As he stared forward, looking at the exterior of the ship moving away from him, he remembered the hand that had pinned him down. As his vision shrunk to a pin, before going black, he got a glimpse of Jason standing in the docking bay, waving.

His vision was gone.

...

Something bumped Rick's head.

Rick opened his eyes to see that he was still in the docking bay, the doors were still closed, and he had floated away from the shuttle. He had just had a hallucination. He looked around, his skin was normal, his vision focused, and he was alone. He knew what Taisha would say. It was a result of inconsistent sleep, malnutrition, and extreme emotional trauma. If he didn't take care of himself soon, then he wouldn't last long enough to make it to Shadow

Space Colony for final review, let alone finish the mission.

Rick pulled some fruit out of his pocket with a thin and pale hand and ate it quickly. He replaced the items Tim had questioned as fast as he could. After several hours of work he attempted to turn on the engines and they fired immediately. The shuttle was fixed and without taking time to revel in his accomplishment Rick left the docking bay as quickly as he could.

24 May 2338
Chapter 14

Rick picked up the towel next to him and wiped the sweat away from his eyes. He breathed heavily from exhaustion as he put his weights into their locks.

Since his hallucination in the docking bay, Rick had made sure to exercise and eat well to get healthier. He also took sleeping pills to try and stay rested. He had not had any more hallucinations, and his renewed energy allowed his dreams to take on a more positive tone. He often dreamed about the tasks ahead of him. There was great relief when he looked in the mirror recently and saw his face was fuller. The color of his skin was not so pale, and his hair was becoming thicker again.

The ship had reached full speed two days ago and Rick had intended to be in the sleep chamber soon after, but he was surprised at how much preparation was still needed before he went to sleep. He knew it also provided him with more time to prepare himself physically for his stasis. He had only a little gardening and a few ship systems to review for the day, and he would be ready for sleep.

Rick walked to the teleporter, placed his wet towel on the pad, and sent the towel to his house so he could wash it. He then used the teleporter to jump to engineering so he could enter the room with the mass accelerator. As he walked to the entrance, he whistled loudly. Most areas of the ship were large and open. His whistle bounced nicely off the walls. He had picked up the habit of whistling a few days earlier when he realized that the echo made the room feel less empty and helped him not feel alone.

He moved into the mass accelerator room and was surprised by how small the area felt. Jason had been the only one to go into the room while at full speed and it looked completely different than what Rick had seen last.

The room ended at a glass wall directly behind the control panel. On the other side of the glass was pure black. Rick knew how to read the control panel and had been trained to fix minor issues with the accelerators, but the majority of how they worked remained a mystery to him.

He knew that the two cores, at the end of each prong of the ship, worked together to create a tidal wave of light. The ship rode inside a sort of bubble within the wave that allowed the ship to travel at nearly the speed of light. The glass behind the control panel was actually a one-way mirror, but when the core was at full speed it absorbed all light and nothing could be seen.

Rick checked the gauges on the control panel. Everything was running as intended. The log showed that the ship had already encountered a solar wave and the new panels the crew had installed worked perfectly.

He knew that if Jason were doing this maintenance check, he would likely be in here for a while, but Rick still found it difficult to spend more time in a room that the others primarily used than he had to. He quickly looked around the room before leaving and noticed a wrench on the floor. He picked up the wrench and examined it. It was completely clean and showed no signs of wear. It was likely that whatever it had been used for last was it's first time out of the packaging, thought Rick.

He began whistling as he exited the mass accelerator room into engineering. He walked over to a nearby drawer and placed the wrench inside. It quickly snapped to the magnetic bottom of the drawer. He continued walking to the crew facilities, examining the area as he went. Nothing was out of place. He took the time to notice the change in the echo of his whistle as he walked from engineering to the crew facilities.

Rick did not bother examining the crew area because he had already done it several days ago. He continued walking to the Agrosim so he could finish his gardening.

As he entered the Agrosim he noticed that there was less work to do than he had expected. *The machinery must have been fixed*, thought Rick. He retrieved his gardening tools and trimmed the few branches that were still too low for the machines to reach. In less than an hour he had finished the remaining gardening. He made sure to examine the machines to confirm that there were no potential risks for them. The machines were clean and their tracks were clear of debris and the branches of tall trees.

. . .

Rick lingered as he put his laundry into the washer. He had realized on the way back to his house that he had never checked the other homes for anything that needed to be cleaned before he entered the sleep chamber. He knew he had to deal with the issue. In a closed off environment, air filters would not do enough for him to ignore the situation. He decided to address the issue as quickly as possible and not allow himself to dwell on it. He finished starting his laundry and left his home.

Rick looked at the open area. The east and west walls each had ten apartments on them. In what little exposure he had to the world outside of school and HIEPE he had never seen such large apartments. The size of them reminded him of townhouses, or what he imagined a wealthy New Yorker might live in, though not nearly as fancy. Each apartment was three stories tall, had three bedrooms and an office, and the third floor was dedicated to storage. They all had large kitchens as well because they were designed to have many people living in them at once after the ship arrived on the new planet, and scientists needed a place to live while preparing the planet for human life.

He would start with Tim and Linda's house because it was the farthest away. The difference in distance, he knew, was insignificant, but he felt better about working toward his home rather than away from it. For the past week he had been going throughout the ship with minimal issues. However, now faced with the idea of being forced to confront his emotions with no one to support him, he felt very alone. At the same time, the prospect of going into the crews' private quarters left him somehow stricken with a conflicting feeling as though he were being watched. The distance seemed magnified as he moved toward their apartment.

Rick rested his hand on the door handle and slowly turned it. The only doors on the ship that had locks were bedroom and bathroom doors. Just as much as he felt open and exposed as he walked from his apartment to here, he instantly felt claustrophobic as he looked into the empty space. The only lights that could be seen were from various electronics and the fire alarm overhead.

Rick quickly turned on the lights and ran up the stairs to the top floor so he could work from the top to the bottom. He knew exactly what he needed to do, dispose of all waste and unplug all electronics. Unplugging electronics wasn't standard, but he knew they would only waste electricity and be a potential source of fire.

He opened the door to the storage and flicked the lights on. He glanced around and found nothing out of place. He then moved to the second floor and checked the three bedrooms and bathroom. He unplugged all the clocks and lamps in each room, and emptied a bottle of water he found into the sink.

Finally, he checked the bottom floor. All the rooms downstairs were spotless. He unplugged everything he could find and left the house as quickly as possible. Relief briefly ran through him after finishing one apartment without issues.

He went to the apartment across from his, which belonged to Jason and Taisha. Their apartment was as uneventful as the first one had been, and he was pleased with how quickly he was making progress.

The last apartment was next to his. He rested his hand on the door handle and took a deep breath. Other than Jessica, Matt was the one he missed most.

While most of the crew had been too busy with their various tasks and the sleep chambers, Adelina had made a point of making her home her own as quickly as possible. The other apartments still had most of their moving boxes stashed in the attics, to be tended to at a later date. However, it had always been important to Adelina to photograph events and she displayed those photographs throughout their home. He knew he would have to confront the issue eventually, but he wasn't ready to look at pictures yet, to be forced to remember.

Rick opened the door, flicked the lights on, and bolted up the stairs while looking toward the floor. The storage was the same as the others. The second floor was clean and Rick was able to inspect it without looking higher than table level. All that remained was the bottom floor and he would be done.

Rick quickly inspected the living room as he made his way to the kitchen. Both rooms were clean and Rick made sure to unplug all the appliances. The only room that still needed inspection was the office. Rick remembered that Adelina kept many of her photos in the office, but he was determined to stay focused. As long as he was quick, it would be easy, he assured himself.

From the hallway, Rick reached around the door frame and turned the light on. He then whipped through the door, scanned the floor and desktops, and immediately turned the lights off. He paused for a moment in the dark, sorting out what he had just seen. He hadn't noticed anything that needed attention. Then, as he stood there, his eyes slowly adjusted to the dark, and he noticed the faint red glow of a clock.

Carefully Rick walked into the dark room toward the glow coming from Adelina's desk. He tried to see where the clock was plugged in, but the light that it released seemed to be swallowed by darkness before illuminating the area around it. He reached around to the back of the clock and started to follow the cord to its source. The cord ran behind several pictures that Rick knocked over as he followed its path that eventually led behind the desk.

Dropping onto his hands and knees, he crawled into the leg space of the desk. Reaching behind the desk, he ran his hand along the wall in an attempt to find the outlet. Finally locating the outlet, he pulled out the plug. As he brought his hand back from behind the desk, his wedding ring became caught on something and slid off of his finger. Rick sat up quickly in shock, hitting his head hard on the bottom of the desk as he heard his ring hit the ground and roll. He heard several things fall over from the impact of his head, which hurt fiercely from the blow.

Rick lay on the floor in the pitch black office for several minutes. He debated with himself on how important the ring was to him. He knew he would have to turn the lights on to find it.

He stood up and moved to the light switch. He didn't feel right about not wearing his ring, and he justified the trouble he was putting himself through by telling himself that the ring could be lost forever if gravity had to be turned off in an emergency.

With a sigh, Rick turned the lights on, glancing at Adelina's desk as he threw his vision to the ground. Several pictures had been knocked over by him and one hung partially over the edge of the desk. He walked over to where he had been lying and got onto the floor, laying his head on the ground so that he could peer under the desk. He saw that the ring had rolled away from where he was, but was still close enough that he might have been able to reach it.

Rick slid his arm under the desk, stretching his fingers

out to reach his ring. The tips of his fingers lightly grazed the edge of the ring, but Rick was careful not to accidentally push it further away. He shoved his body toward the desk to try to reach farther, knocking the image that had been hanging over the side of the desk to the ground. With one full extension of his arm and fingers he flicked the ring and it rolled closer so that he could easily retrieve it.

As Rick began backing out from underneath the desk, his hand fell upon the picture that lay on the ground. Without thinking, he picked up the image to put it on the desk. As he did so, he saw a portrait of Jessica.

A month before they left on their mission, it had been Adelina's birthday. Because of her love for photographs, each person had taken a portrait of themselves and written a message to her on the back.

Jessica's smile was striking. She had been on the verge of laughing. The photo shoot that the crew had partaken in had been filled with laughter, which had given each photo a stronger sense of authenticity. Her flowing, wavy hair was draped over her left shoulder onto her chest like a sash, and her vibrant green eyes sparkled in a way that Rick wouldn't have believed a photograph could capture if he weren't currently looking at it.

Rick's heart broke as he stared at the picture. As much as it hurt, he felt foolish for fearing this moment so strongly. He began setting up the pictures that he had knocked over on the desk. The pictures that lined her desk were the portraits they had taken, including the portrait of Adelina that Matt demanded she take on her birthday. When all the images were set up, Rick took a step back, and froze as he noticed the images, his crew, staring back at him.

24 June 2338
Chapter 15

The lid of the sleep chamber swung open and a blaring alarm pierced Rick's ears, waking him so quickly that he threw himself to his feet. The lights were dim. The emergency lighting offered just enough light that he didn't have to squint. The air was thin and Rick's muscles were weak from the sleep chamber. He grabbed an oxygen mask and attached the bottle to a belt loop with a clip. Taking deep breaths, the oxygen slowly relieved the burning his muscles felt as he forced himself to exert his body more than it was ready for.

The computer monitor showed that there was extreme overheating in engine room A. Rick made his way to the teleporter until he noticed that it was powered off. As he ran down the stairs toward his front door, he debated what he should do. He could control most things on the ship from the cockpit, but he may not have time to get to the engine room from the cockpit if he had to do something manually.

As he reached his front door, he decided that he had more options from the cockpit and could better assess the situation. Smoke rushed in as he opened the door. The open area was filled with smoke. It was darker than Rick was expecting. The emergency lighting was not working properly, thought Rick. As he took a moment to orient himself, he noticed moving shadows toward the Agrosim. He knew there was nothing that could be moving in that area. Confusion and curiosity moved him in the shadows' direction to investigate. As he walked forward, squinting fiercely, the shadows appeared to be getting farther away.

Rick followed the shadows into the Agrosim. The humid air made black streaks on his skin from the smoke. The smoke swirled in the air around the branches that stirred it as they swayed. Their movements were too extreme to be natural, he noticed. Someone had come through here. He looked at the ground. It was black and slick from the smoke and humidity. Behind him his footsteps left clear marks. Looking ahead, the black was in long rows. Something had been dragged through the area. He looked for footsteps, but if there had been any, they were covered by whatever had been slid across the floor.

Rick followed the streaks on the floor, which led into engineering. The black streaks were in stark contrast to the immaculate white of the engineering room. The tracks went straight into the engine room. He ran to the door, his foot kicking a wrench that sat just outside of it. An intense heat emanated from the door. The heat made him pause before opening the door. A heat strong enough to breach the door seemed too dangerous, but whoever he was following had been able to enter. His desire for answers was too strong to turn away. He gripped the handle, which burned his skin, and slowly opened the door.

A flood of heat and sulfurous smoke poured over Rick, making the hair on his arms stand on end. His eyes were instantly dry and he threw his hands over his face as he waited for his eyes to water. As the initial wave of heat passed he slowly opened his eyes. From where he stood he could not see if anyone was in the room. All he could see were bright rays of light struggling to escape through the smoke on the opposite side of the protective glass. The smoke moved in a slow circular motion around the core as small cracks of lightning shot out and hit the glass.

Rick stared through the cracks between his fingers in amazement. Only a distant portion of his mind was aware of the pain he was in. As he watched he saw a dark mass moving in the opposite direction of the smoke. He peered through his fingers intently, trying to discern what he was seeing. The mass seemed to get smaller as it moved toward the glass until Rick saw a hand press against it. The hand ran it's fingers across the glass, leaving long streaks of tempestuous smoke. Just as the hand pulled away, lightning shot out from the impetuous core and broke the glass. Instantly a blast of heat escaped through the crack and hit Rick. A new emergency alarm suddenly began and the door in front of him slammed closed automatically.

The skin on the back of his hands, which had been in front of his face to shield his eyes, began to blister from the ferocious wave of heat. His right eye had been peeking between his fingers and had lost its vision with searing pain. As Rick clutched at his eye, it caved slightly under the pressure. He attempted to open his eye, but the lid was glued shut.

Rick let out an agonizing scream even before the shock wore off enough for him to realize what had happened. He coughed on the bit of smoke that had escaped from the core before the door closed.

"Emergency, core 'A' heat levels are at catastrophic limits. Core room 'A' and engineering are compromised and will be ejected in twenty seconds. Evacuate the areas immediately," announced an automated voice over the intercom.

Rick panicked and began running for the exit. As he ran a table struck his right side and he fell to the floor. He struggled to get to his feet, his flesh burning furiously as he moved. He looked around to find the door and saw it as it began to close.

As he made his way to the door the gravity turned off and he floated forward with no control over his momentum. The door was closing too quickly and he knew he wouldn't make it. He reached out his hands in desperation and got an arm through the door right before it closed. He screamed in agony as the door continued to close and, without resistance, severed his arm at the elbow with a loud crunch.

As Rick screamed he no longer noticed his eye. He didn't notice the lights going out or hear the ejection of core 'A' and engineering from the ship. He couldn't tell the difference between his sweat and the blood that rained upon him. He was lost until he felt something that took his mind away from his arm.

He knew he was going to die, not from his arm, but from the heat emanating from the door leading to the core, which had opened when the power shut off. As his body started to go cold, while his flesh and nerves melted away, the core exploded.

26 March 2340
Chapter 16

Rick let out a deep sigh. Over the past two years he had grown to hate the sleep chamber. He considered himself lucky when he had a dream as extreme as the one he just had. He was continually having a harder time distinguishing between his dreams and reality, so any dream that was as physically harming as this last one was easy to disconnect from.

He took his time getting up. Today he was supposed to begin slowing the ship down, but he had not yet figured out what to do about Shadow Space Colony. He wasn't sure if he could keep people on the station from finding out that he did not have a crew. Considering the radio conversation he had last time the ship was stopped, he wasn't sure there was anything that would prevent them from trying to take the ship if they found out. The flip side was that he could potentially recruit a new crew, people that could help him not to be isolated and could even be trained to assist with the ship's maintenance.

Will I be able to trust a new crew? Would their lack of knowledge and experience hurt the mission more than it would help it? Can I acquire a new crew without risking the ship or the mission? The questions seemed unanswerable and yet circled through his mind endlessly. As much as he hated the risk of stopping at all, he felt as though he had no choice. The new teleporter, according to Dr. Rodriguez, was critical to the maintenance and survival of Shadow Space Colony, and he knew he couldn't betray them simply to protect his own ambitions.

Rick sat up and swung his feet over the side of the bed. His legs tingled as he moved them, as though they were asleep. As the tingling went away, his muscles began to tighten. He massaged them quickly before it became painful. During the past two years he had spent significantly less time awake than his body needed. He feared having to deal with the effects of isolation, so he only spent three or four days awake at a time. He had only been awake for a total of two weeks, hardly enough time to struggle with isolation. During the times that Rick was awake he tried to stay distracted, and the next six weeks should make that easy. He was overwhelmed with anxiety for his visit to Shadow Space Colony.

Rick walked out of his room and went down the stairs slowly. He was exhausted quickly by his weak muscles. He began whistling as he left his house and took time to notice the change in the reverberation as he walked into the open path leading to the cockpit. He could see the lights ahead of him turning on in anticipation of his arrival. The lights always stayed on, except when he was in the sleep chamber, they turned back on with motion detectors.

In the cockpit the screens came alive as Rick entered. He checked the ship's status and logs and found nothing unusual. Not being able to think of a reason to stall any longer, he walked to a console and initiated the deceleration procedure. A clock appeared on the screen in front of him with an estimated stop date. He had six weeks and one day to devise a plan for Shadow Space Colony.

. . .

"And then he turned, and walked back toward the entrance of the hotel. The end," said a confident male voice over the intercom.

A week ago, Rick had been reviewing the inventory in preparation for Shadow Space Colony and came across a collection of ancient classical literature translated into modern English as audio books. They helped fight the feeling of loneliness and allowed him to appreciate silence when there was some. The recording had just finished *Jurassic Park* by Michael Crichton. He enjoyed classical literature because of his amusement with what previous generations thought would happen in science.

"Incoming radio transmission," announced an automated voice over the intercom.

Rick set down the weights he had been lifting. He used the towel next to him to wipe his face and the bench he had laid on. At the teleporter he sent the towel to his house and then jumped to the cockpit.

"Incoming radio transmission," repeated the voice.

"Accept transmission," responded Rick, his stomach in knots. He quickly flexed his muscles and let out a grunt. He needed to feel confident so he could sound confident.

A chime rang indicating the call was initiated.

"This is Captain Lanson speaking," said Rick.

Rick could hear some snickering in the background. "Oh, uh, yes. This is General Smith of Shadow Space Colony, speaking on behalf of his crew. Do you plan to dock here, *Captain*?" The laughing in the background exploded.

"What's so funny?" asked Rick, irritated.

"Ha! Sorry, we just love having fun with new people, they always seem to take titles so seriously. Around here, we don't judge a man by his title, but by his actions."

"Well, then by your standards I'm sure you can understand why I would be less than impressed with you right now," replied Rick, immediately annoyed.

"Oooh, we better watch out boys, we got a sharp one here!" General Smith said to his crew. Rick could hear several men, their laughter slowly dying. "Now what's your name, so I know what to call you?"

"My name is Rick. Isn't my information on file?"

"I don't know, probably. I'll be honest with you. I only knew you were coming because a couple of days ago a message popped up on my screen telling me to expect visitors. If there is a file, then my Grandpa would be the one to talk to since he would have been the one to file it forty years ago. I gotta say, the whole station is interested to meet people and see the ship that traveled from Earth. There isn't a person alive who can remember the last time that happened. We haven't even seen any new faces in years. From what our scanners are showing, it looks like you are a couple of days away. Now that we've made contact with you I'll tell the crew to dust off the docking bay in preparation for your arrival."

"I'd like to unload your supplies as quickly as possible so that I can fire the engines back up, while they are still warm," said Rick as an excuse to not stay long. He knew that the longer he was there, the more time they had to find out that he lacked a crew.

"We like to take our time around here, what I like to refer

to as an outer space version of island time, and I don't want anyone getting hurt while moving the supplies. But I'll let them know, the *Captain* said to be quick," replied the man sarcastically as he ended the call.

Rick's anxiety grew. He did not have a good feeling about Shadow Space Colony.

. . .

"The estimated time of arrival is three hours," announced the automated female voice over the intercom.

Two hours ago, Rick realized that not all of the supplies for Shadow Space Colony were in the docking bay like they should have been. He had been scrambling ever since to get everything ready before he arrived. He had moved all the things he could, but several things would have been difficult for multiple people and were impossible for one. He would have to turn gravity off to move the heaviest objects.

Rick took a deep breath before he slammed his hand down on the button to turn gravity off.

"Please secure all loose items. Gravity will go off in thirty seconds," announced a female voice over the intercom.

Rick let out a sigh. "I'm not going to make it." Beads of sweat dripped down his face as he waited anxiously for gravity to turn off. He looked down at his hands, which had turned white. He relaxed his grip on the dolly he was going to use for the cargo. He reached down and turned on the thrusters that would allow him to steer.

A loud buzzer rang over the intercom as a voice announced, "The gravity is now deactivated."

The buzzing continued in pulses as gravity slowly lifted

and the dolly rose off the ground. By going back and forth from the cockpit Rick had learned to no longer notice the falling feeling he got when entering zero gravity. He fired the thrusters on the dolly and propelled himself forward. The cargo room was large and fortunately the computer had been able to bring him everything he needed without him having to search for it. The massive crate before him contained a large teleporter that would allow for large building materials to be teleported. Previous models of teleporters could not send the quantum connections contained within the new teleporter, so the new teleporter had to be delivered manually.

Rick shoved against the 300kg crate to lift it slightly off the ground. He quickly moved the dolly underneath and scrambled to attach the straps before the crate could drift too far away. Once the crate was strapped down, he fired the dolly's thrusters lightly to move the cargo forward. He had to resist the urge to rush himself. It was difficult to steer from behind the large crate, but he knew better than to pull the crate behind him. Even at a low speed, a 300kg crate would crush him without friction to slow it down.

Rick moved forward slowly. He had one more crate to move after this and he knew it would be close trying to get it done before reaching Shadow Space Colony, but it was possible. He whistled loudly to fight the anxiety he felt by having to move slowly. The noise hit the wood crate and bounced directly at him. The path he needed to travel was a straight line. He gauged his location by the view next to him, only peaking around the crate to see what was in front of it occasionally.

It took just over an hour to move the crate and set it into

position. The most difficult part was navigating the turn through the tunnel into the docking bay. The transportation went without issue. Rick now waited for the computer in inventory to bring the second crate forward. His whistle died off into the distance of the room. He no longer noticed what he whistled, only how the sound interacted with the room around him.

The crate was lowered into position from above. Rick placed the dolly so the crate landed on top. He quickly tied the straps and fired the thrusters to move forward. He moved more quickly with this crate. He wanted to move it to the docking bay with enough time to make sure he hadn't forgotten anything.

He reached the end of Maintenance and fired the thrusters as he entered Medical. The right thruster shot out a spark and the light it emitted dimmed. The crate turned right sharply, forcing him to fire the thrusters in reverse. The crate straightened out and slowly came to a stop.

He looked at his watch. He had thirty minutes left. He fired the thrusters lightly. They both fired with the same intensity. He fired them again with more force and the left lit with full force while the right stayed low. The crate turned sharp to the right and Rick quickly hit reverse and brought the crate to a stop.

Rick knew he would have to go slower than he wanted. Even if he gradually built up speed, the crate would turn if he tried to stop too quickly. He triggered the thrusters lightly. The crate gradually moved forward. He moved slowly through Medical, growing more anxious as the minutes passed. He whistled loudly and listened.

Rick stopped.

He looked around at his surroundings, saw the open path to Maintenance behind him. He whistled again and listened. The noise did not die out behind him like he expected, but seemed to bounce back to him. He stopped whistling. The whistling continued from behind him.

Rick froze and listened. He did not recognize the melody. The notes were long, a little shaky, and getting louder. He looked back and scanned the environment, trying to find the source. Suddenly, in the distance, the lights went out and the area was consumed with an unnatural darkness that reminded Rick of the other side of the glass wall in the engine room. Then the lights in front of him went out and darkness came closer. The darkness continued to make its way toward him as each row of lights went out.

Rick panicked and accelerated the dolly. The dolly turned sharply to the right and crashed into the wall. He slammed into the crate and bounced away. The crate rolled over, turning the dolly upside down. Rick pushed himself off of a nearby surface as the crate drifted toward the tunnel leading to the docking bay. He looked at the tunnel, which, from the upside down, now turned to the right.

Rick took control of his fear and formulated a plan. He accelerated the dolly just hard enough that it turned with the curve of the tunnel. Just as the door to the docking bay came into sight, the lights around him went out. The distance to the door suddenly felt significant. The light from the door struggled to breach the darkness that surrounded Rick. He focused his direction on the door. He felt as though he was moving painfully slowly. As he desperately struggled to reach the door, he became aware again of the whistling that now sounded like it was right behind him. He was sure that if he reached back he would touch his pursuer.

Everything appeared to be in slow motion. Rick was moving too fast to enter the docking bay. With sudden ease and gracefulness, he slammed in reverse. The crate came to a dead stop and spun left sharply. Right before the crate faced the door, he gunned the dolly forward. The crate stopped spinning and shot forward through the door. The crate crashed into an anchored table making Rick lose his grip on the dolly and hit head-first into the crate.

08 May 2340

Chapter 17

"Transmission requested."

The crate Rick had been pushing lingered peacefully, inches above the ground, not moving. He could see light in the tunnel and flashing lights from the control panel in the cockpit. He felt where he had hit his head. There was no bump and he felt no pain.

"Transmission requested," repeated the computer over the intercom.

Rick pushed himself off of a nearby table and floated into the cockpit. "This is the Captain speaking."

"Wow, you're alive! We were starting to think you were dead and we would have to force our way in. What took you so long? We've been waiting for over thirty minutes," said Smith.

"I, uh … we were having issues with our radio that we had to fix," replied Rick.

Smith responded dryly. "You guys are in charge of a ship with technology that can travel at the speed of light and it took you thirty minutes to fix the radio? You should be able to build a new one in that time! Anyway, you could have just opened the door and gone outside, we're right here."

"I'll open the bay doors right after I put my space suit on."

"I gather together an entire team to move this stuff as quickly as possible, as per your request, and we have been waiting outside for over thirty minutes, but, by all means, take your time," replied Smith sharply.

Rick turned off the radio. He felt his head again. There was no indication that he had hit it. He moved out of the cockpit and peered down the tunnel. From what he could see, the lights were on. When he reached the dolly he fired the thrusters, and the crate turned. He reversed it to stop the crate.

He had somehow moved the crate successfully, despite a broken thruster, while hallucinating. He knew he didn't have time to figure out how or why it happened. He got dressed quickly and closed the air lock leading into the ship from the docking bay so he could open the bay doors.

Rick worked quickly to open both bay doors at the same time. Alarms blared initially, warning of the dangers of having both doors opened concurrently. He overrode them. He knew his best argument for preventing visitors from exploring the rest of the ship was by requiring that the airlock to the rest of the ship remain closed.

Slowly the bay doors opened and revealed the vacuumous space beyond. The safe and familiar bounds of the ship dropping off into the inhospitable void reminded him of aerial views of islands where the island below the water would suddenly drop away into the menacingly dark blue of the deep ocean. A dread sunk into his bones, that he was standing on the edge of a cliff that led to a world he was not meant to enter.

The shuttle of his visitors emerged from the black ocean outside, and he couldn't help but associate them with the dangerous creatures of the deep ocean. Eventually the shuttle door opened.

"For someone so concerned about speed, you sure do take your time," said a round man as he floated out of his shuttle. "I'm General Smith. We talked on the radio. I'm guessing that you are Captain Lanson?" The man's jowls, covered in gray stubble, filled his helmet in a way that made Rick feel claustrophobic simply by looking at him. His eyes were ominously cast in shadow, making Rick feel that he needed to remain on guard.

"Yes sir, General."

General Smith burst into laughter that crackled over the short range radio in Rick's helmet. "Dang it! I couldn't play it cool for five minutes. Now I owe Dan ten bucks!" He moved over to where Rick was and put his hand on Rick's shoulder. "I told you before, Rick, we don't care about titles here. The name is Jamie Smith, but you can call me Smith. I can't change the fact that my parents gave me a girl's name, but if you say it, even once, I will put you down."

Two men came out of the shuttle and began examining the crates that Rick had sectioned off for them.

"Are these all the men you brought?" asked Rick.

"You bet, and I had a hell of a time gathering them together. We haven't had a crew to maintain the docking bay or for moving equipment for as long as I've been alive." Smith looked around for a moment. "Speaking of crews, where is yours?"

Rick's stomach dropped. He had planned for this moment. He did his best to mimic Smith's demeanor. "Are you kidding me? We have been isolated on this ship for over four years, and the world around us has had eighty years to develop new diseases. Our immune systems are not prepared for this encounter. I'm going to be quarantined for two weeks after this to make sure no one gets sick. Besides, this ship doesn't stop very often. They have work to do and don't have time to gab it up with your friends here," said Rick with surprising force. "Not to mention that, to get the equipment out, I have to have both bay doors open and seal the door to the ship. They wouldn't get anything done if they had to wear space suits just so they could be here to say hello."

"I guess that means I'm not getting a tour then," said Smith with a disingenuously sad face. He looked at the crates and then at their shuttle. "It looks like we're going to need to make multiple trips."

The two men let out small groans.

"They're going to be a while, and I can't stand being in this suit. How about you escort me back to the station in your shuttle, Rick?" asked Smith.

"I'd actually prefer to stay here. I have things to do," replied Rick.

"It'll be fine. You have plenty of time. Anyway, it's not that often that we have a visitor or a delivery of this magnitude, so we have the standard paperwork that needs to get filled out. You know how it is. Plus, I really want to get out of this suit." Smith pawed at his stomach to express his discomfort from the clearly tight suit. He began moving toward Rick's shuttle.

"I really don't see why I need to fill out paperwork. If you just need something to say I was here, then I think the cargo being here will suffice," said Rick nervously.

"Isolation must really mess with a person because you are acting weird. If I didn't know any better, I would think something was wrong. Is there anything you need to tell me?" asked Smith.

"No, no," snapped Rick. "You know how it is. If I'm not here cracking the whip, then no work gets done. But I guess I can spare a few minutes, as long as we're quick."

"These guys aren't exactly the fastest workers, and they will have to make several trips, so we have time to spare. I'll show you around a bit," said Smith with a grin.

...

Rick moved out of the shuttle into an exposed docking area on the exterior of the station. It reminded him of parking a car on the curb back on Earth, though the sidewalk here was lined with hand rails.

"Do you have any ropes for me to clip on to?" asked Rick.

"What, so you don't float away? We don't worry about ropes. We have life guards at every exit of the station. If someone floats away, lifeguards can retrieve that person before he can get far. We also found that we had fewer accidents when we got rid of the ropes. People became much more careful when they had something to worry about," said Smith.

Rick grabbed onto the rail with a tight grip. He looked back at his ship that rested a hundred meters away from the station. He had always been amazed by the size of his ship. It was designed to support a hundred scientists once it reached the new planet. While early settlers could take the risk of colonizing on the surface of an unknown planet, the scientists would have a safe, self-sustaining environment to take refuge in while they conditioned the planet for human life. However, as he had been flying toward Shadow Space Colony, he quickly realized how small his ship was in comparison. Shadow Space Colony was seven times larger and was designed for a much denser population.

"How many people live here?" asked Rick.

"Around 1300," replied Smith.

"Wow, how many people can this station support?"

"Around 1300," answered Smith, grimly.

Rick saw a sign above the door they were entering which read "Transfer." As they floated into a small room he saw another sign "All suits must remain air tight while in the transfer room. Lack of adherence may result in death." A low swish sound could be heard as the room became pressurized.

"That seems risky. What happens if there is a sudden increase in population? How do you control resource distribution?" asked Rick.

"It didn't use to be this way. Eighty years ago, when you left Earth, people could come and go as they pleased. We maintained a population of around eight hundred. But, as you may remember, even before you left, there began to be tension on Earth over resources. Turns out, the estimated time span for resource consumption might have been a little high. It was based on an individual who consumed just enough to survive, not to be full. It also did not take into consideration hoarding, or the consequences of hoarding.

A thousand years of supplies can vanish quickly when individuals take three or four times what they need. Now the ones who have extra actually consume more than they would normally because it is so readily available and because that availability prevents them from seeing how dire things really are. The other problem with hoarding is that those who have not try to take from those who have. When enough people do not succeed in taking what they want, they often decide to destroy that item so no one can have it. Farms that were heavily guarded would be set on fire, killing the farmers who would not share and destroying the crops."

With the air levels raised, the door in front of them opened, exposing a hallway with many doors on each side. The hallway, a sterile white, appeared undecorated and grungy, which Rick assumed was from the difficulty of getting supplies to such a remote location.

"How much time do you think Earth has left?" asked Rick calmly.

"It's not as bad as you might think. With all the killing and starvation, people are almost dying faster than the rate of consumption. I think the predicted date for full resource exhaustion will end up being fairly accurate no matter what. The real question will be how many people will be alive when that day comes."

"But that day is so far away, I'm sure that things will calm down once the novelty of that prediction wears off," said Rick.

After walking through a series of depressing hallways with doors on each side, they finally reached an office where Smith stopped. The door had "Shadow Space Colony Traffic Control" written on it. Inside the office were many file cabinets, a desk, and some chairs, which Rick sat himself in. The back of the office was lined with windows that overlooked a large community area that appeared to have sunlight and a simulated sky above them. From where he sat he could tell they were at least ten stories up.

"Normally I would agree with you, that everything would blow over soon, but nations don't react like individuals. They care about the longevity of their people well beyond the lifespan of a single person, rarely because of compassion mind you, let's not kid ourselves. It's all about legacy, fame, whatever you want to call it. But when people think of World War II, they always think about the genocide, but they forget entirely about the fact that Hitler was also scared for the environment. The actual war was for the expansion of land, which was because he was afraid of dwindling resources. Now, that fear is actually true. Don't get me wrong, they also care about power, and the power of controlling resources like this has never been stronger. For our sake, though, I hope you're right. These are difficult times. We had to turn off our portal to protect ourselves from those who wanted to take over this colony, and our population has climbed ever since. Being able to open the portal up again would relieve a significant burden," said Smith.

"Is there anything you can do to try and control the growth of your population?"

Smith leaned back in his chair, the stubbly fat around his face consuming his chin. "Nothing traditional."

"What do you mean?"

"We don't exactly have any way to produce birth control around here, and the uproar that occurred when we tried separating the genders made that option impossible. They're like teenagers. You were a teenager once, you know how it works. Tell a bunch of people that they have to stop having sex and they'll end up having more sex than if you had said nothing."

Smith reached for a clipboard that lay on the desk in front of him. He handed it to Rick. "Please sign your name and give a brief description of the nature of your visit."

Rick examined the paper.

"It's just a formality, you know how it is." Smith paused for a moment as Rick began to write. "One thing that has kept the population down is our enforcement of laws. If there is a fight between two people, we let it play out until only one person is left. If the person who started the fight is the one left standing, then he must suffer the same punishment that all other crimes receive.

Anyone who commits a crime is forced to excavate local planets for resources to bring back to the colony. There is about a thirty percent survival rate. If you survive then your punishment is paid. However, the death penalty has been enacted upon the fourth criminal offense." Smith stood as Rick finished filling out the paperwork. He glanced at his watch. "I'm sure my boys are just about done."

Rick stood and followed Smith out of his office. "With such severe punishments, you must have low crime rates."

"Ha! No! We have a population almost under control. Crime always follows poverty, and as the years passed, we all became poor," responded Smith.

Rick took a quick glance at Smith's large stomach that stretched his space suit tight. "These times must be very difficult for you," said Rick dryly.

"Ha ha! I suffer for my people in spirit!" replied Smith, noticing Rick's glance. "I cannot be expected to give a fair and honest judgment on an empty stomach. I must be sharp and aware so that I may best serve others."

Rick walked in silence. He decided it was best to not upset Smith. As the two men walked back to his shuttle, he noticed how everyone they passed seemed to avoid Smith. No one looked at him and everyone moved out of his way as he approached. Rick was getting the feeling that interacting with Smith put him in more danger than he had previously suspected.

Finally, they reached the transfer room. Rick secured his helmet and stepped inside. The two men stood inside, waiting for the air to be sucked out of the room. Smith looked at his watch and tapped the radio built into his helmet. "I was expecting to hear back from my crew, but these short distance radios don't work very well when inside the colony," said Smith.

"So is anyone working on a long term solution to the current situation at the station?" asked Rick.

The door to the exterior opened and they continued toward the shuttle.

"Not really, though we do acquire new technology where …" Smith paused and listened to the radio in his helmet.

As Rick waited he could see the cargo being removed from the shuttle that Smith had used to get to his ship from Shadow Space Colony. Smith gave short replies and appeared very focused.

"Sorry about that," said Smith. He stared out at Rick's ship. "That sure is a large ship. It must be difficult to maintain."

Rick was surprised by how calmly Smith acted immediately after appearing to have had a serious conversation over the radio. "Most things on the ship are automated. It's very easy to maintain," replied Rick.

"I read that ship can sustain up to two hundred people," said Smith as he turned to look at Rick with a cold, determined stare.

Rick's body became tense. "That number is only a guess,

since it's never been tested. However many it may be, it pales in comparison to the number of lives the new planet could save."

"Who are you kidding? There is no way to know if anyone will still be alive by the time you get there, if the planet will actually be able to support life, or if the ship can actually make the journey. There are people here, right now, who could use the resources. We need that ship to survive," said Smith bluntly.

"Don't be so short-sighted. All things in life come with risk, a chance for failure, but that doesn't mean we shouldn't try. Everyone is suffering right now and this ship can't stop that, but the new planet could," replied Rick.

Smith's anger boiled quickly, his face contorting as he struggled to absorb Rick's defiance. "So we have to just stay here and die while you live on a ship built for two hundred, *alone*?"

Shock consumed Rick as the discovery of his secret was revealed. Immediately Rick shoved Smith. The force sent Smith flying away and pushed Rick toward his shuttle. The two men unloading the nearby shuttle moved to catch Smith.

"No you idiots! Don't let him leave!" barked Smith.

One man continued on course to catch Smith, while the other man pushed off of a nearby railing and threw himself toward Rick. Rick managed to enter his shuttle and lock the door before the man reached him. He looked at the man that was beating on the door. He was not one of the two men who had been on his ship.

Rick quickly fired up the engine and moved away from the commotion outside the shuttle. The three men moved to the shuttle that was being unloaded. Rick could see that the crate they were unloading was only half out. They would have to finish moving it before giving chase to him. Smith beat his fists on the railing nearby.

Rick watched Smith as the shuttle moved toward the ship. Smith stopped moving. A chime rang over the intercom, followed by, "Incoming radio transmission." Rick turned on the radio.

"Rick, I think you might have overreacted to what I was saying," said Smith with a surprising calmness.

The shuttle moved painfully slowly toward the ship. Rick said nothing.

"Listen Rick, we know the truth. We searched your ship high and low. There is no crew. One man cannot pilot that ship for over a hundred years completely alone. You just won't survive. It's impossible," said Smith.

"I have to at least try. I can't just stay here and die," replied Rick.

"There won't be anyone to save by the time you get there. You are so concerned about helping people, yet if you leave you will help no one and leave hundreds of people to die," Smith's anger was struggling to surface again.

"If you cared about your people then you would not be so fat while they starve to death! I know the truth. You, and whoever could bribe you the most, would live on the ship. Everyone else would still die, and I would be among them."

"I can't help that you killed your crew, Rick. But flying off into the cold depths of space to die can't bring them back."

The sting of the insult gave Rick pause. He didn't reply.

"Listen," said Smith reassuringly. "If it makes you feel any better, they were destined to die. Had you not killed them, then the men that moved the cargo would have. If you turn around now and willingly help us learn how to use the ship, we will spare you and you can live with me on the ship. If you don't turn back, Tommy will take the ship by force when you step out of the shuttle. You may be smart, but we have you cornered, and you are no match for our strength."

Rick let out a sigh. "Alright, you win. I'll play nice." Rick spoke slowly with deep tones of defeat. "Does Tommy have a shuttle or should I pick him up? I don't want anyone pressing any buttons until I show you how to use it."

"You've made a wise decision. You can pick him up."

"Is it just him or are there others? I don't have that many seats here."

An audible *click* was heard as Smith switched channels to talk to someone else. Rick began approaching the docking bay between the two long arms and could see Tommy waiting.

Another *click* as Smith returned. "I've changed my mind, just leave Tommy there and come back now," said Smith firmly. "My boys and I are in our shuttle, and will retrieve him ourselves."

"Don't worry about it. I'm almost there. I can see him right now," said Rick as he continued to approach the docking bay.

"I said no, just leave him there and come back now!" demanded Smith.

"The ship has a lot of buttons and I don't want him breaking anything. Sure, your men were able to figure out how to close the bay doors to gain access to the rest of the ship, but that was lucky. They could have easily killed themselves, I'm sure. I've already agreed to work with you, but I want to make sure the ship is used properly so that it lasts," replied Rick calmly. He slowed the shuttle's approach to as slow as he could manage while still moving forward.

The radio clicked off. Smith had hung up. Rick was less than forty meters from the docking bay and could see Tommy talking. Tommy was nodding his head as he looked at the ground, obviously listening intently.

Finally, he looked up and saw Rick approaching. Rick watched as Tommy stood behind a table and waved for Rick to leave. Rick moved the shuttle forward slowly and gestured for Tommy to get in. Tommy continued to wave at Rick, signaling for him to leave. Rick could see Tommy yelling at him and gesturing furiously to turn around. Finally, as Rick reached a spot to park, Tommy moved out into the open, throwing his arms about angrily.

Rick saw his opportunity and accelerated quickly. The shuttle rammed into Tommy before he could get out of the way and pinned him against the table behind him. The shuttle rocked forward with the impact. Grinding vibrations ran through Rick as the shuttle came to a stop and stayed where it was. Tommy screamed wildly. Rick quickly exited the shuttle to see what had happened.

Tommy banged on the shuttle furiously, unable to apply enough force to move it. Rick could see that both of Tommy's legs were bent in unnatural ways. Rick examined the shuttle, which appeared to have not taken any damage. Tommy gave up trying to move the shuttle and laid his head down, groaning loudly. Rick looked at the gauges on Tommy's suit. His oxygen levels were normal, meaning his suit had not been breached. Rick tapped on Tommy's helmet to get him to face Rick. A couple drops of blood floated inside his helmet.

"Can you hear me?" shouted Rick over the man's grunts of pain.

The man nodded his head.

"Both of your legs are broken. The gauges on your suit show that it has not been punctured, though that could change when I move the shuttle."

A look of fear shot through the man's eyes.

"The good news is that there is very little blood in your helmet, so it's likely that most of the damage is internal. However, that also could change when I move the shuttle." Rick could see the fear in the man's face. He was shaking. "Unfortunately, Tommy, I've got to go while I still can and I'm not taking you with me. So we'll just have to risk it and see what happens. Can you speak?"

Tommy gathered his strength and through clenched teeth, said, "Yes." The voice was clear in Rick's helmet.

"Good. I'm sure your friends are coming as quickly as they can. You better let them know to pick you up."

Tommy reached for and turned his radio on. "I'm injured and I need hel... ahhhh."

Rick pushed against the shuttle to dislodge it from the table and it slowly began floating away. Tommy screamed as he came free. Rick grabbed the man, looked him dead in the eyes, "You better keep screaming for help so they can find you." With that, he pushed himself off the end of the table and shoved the man toward the exit. The man tried desperately to grab on to Rick, but he could not get a grip.

Seeing that the man had nothing to grab onto, Rick moved toward the shuttle so he could lock it down. It only took a moment, and as Rick exited the shuttle and looked out, he could see that a shuttle was approaching and that Tommy, now moving far away, was waving his arms to flag them down.

"Incoming radio transmission," announced the computer over his headset.

Rick closed the docking bay doors and moved to the cockpit. He turned on the monitors and switched to the external cameras so he could watch the shuttle. It was halfway down the arms of the ship toward the docking bay. Two men were in the process of retrieving Tommy. Rick turned on the radio.

"Think of all the people you could help if you stayed, Rick," his voice straining to sound calm.

"I'm not buying it, Jamie. We both know you aren't going to help anyone but yourself," replied Rick.

There was a long pause. Rick turned on the engines to warm them up.

"Think of everything you're giving up by leaving," said Smith sternly. "If you leave you are going to die alone and your mission is destined to fail. Listen, you hold all the cards now. If you stay here then you can live like me. I'm never hungry. I can get any substance I want, and I have new women all the time. No one is off limits. You would never be lonely again. You would have all the power you could ever want."

"I would never choose to live like you. You take from those who are too weak to defend themselves. You may say that I am being selfish, but I am sacrificing more than you ever would for the hope of saving future generations. I'm planting a tree whose shade I will never enjoy."

A light on the dashboard signaled that the engines were

ready for firing. Rick watched the monitors as the shuttle turned around to head back to the station.

"You're no savior, Rick. You can't bring them back by sacrificing yourself. You're making a big mistake," said Smith, before turning off the radio.

Rick watched the shuttle leave for a moment. It came close to reaching the end of one of the arms. Rick called the shuttle over the radio.

"What do you want?" asked Smith angrily.

"Jamie, I've decided something," said Rick as he watched the shuttle turn directly behind an arm. "I do want to help your people."

"You're going to stay?" Noticeable doubt was present in Smith's voice.

"No, I'm going to let them have a new leader." Rick pressed the start button to fire the engines. A burst of fire shot out of the ship's exhaust and hit the shuttle. The ship lurched forward under the force. The shuttle was ripped in two and immediately its fuel cells exploded.

Debris shot out in all directions. As the ship moved away from the wreckage, he could faintly see body parts among the remains. He hoped there were no survivors.

14 May 2340
Chapter 18

"Light speed obtained," announced the intercom.

Rick had just finished his fourth sweep of the ship since leaving Shadow Space Colony. He could not escape the feeling that Smith had hidden someone on board. However, two weeks had gone by without any issues and the ships logs showed resource consumption to be normal. Ship surveillance also failed to show any unusual activity. Rick knew his fear was unfounded. He also found it odd that after being isolated for so long that he was afraid that he wasn't alone.

Rick took a deep breath. Reaching full speed meant he would be entering the sleep chamber soon. He began making his way from the cockpit to the cafeteria. Despite his paranoia, he made sure to eat well and exercise. He needed to be in perfect health to withstand the duration in the sleep chamber that he intended to do.

The crew quarters were brightly lit. Normally the lighting would change throughout a twenty-four hour period to emulate day and night, but Rick kept them on their brightest setting at all times. He didn't want anyone to sneak up on him within any shadows. However, he had started noticing streaks of light in his peripheral vision which he assumed was a side effect of the constant light. It had taken a while, but he was also starting to notice the effects of skipping night time. He had slowly adjusted to a thirty hour day and night cycle which felt very natural, but he feared that it was slowing his perception of time. Tasks that should have, and in fact felt as though they had, taken only a few minutes would end up taking over an hour. He knew he would need to restore the light schedule upon waking from the sleep chamber.

Rick picked up the sheers that lay next to the entrance to the Agrosim. He trimmed branches as he moved through the room. The branches had grown out more than he liked, because he had avoided the Agrosim as much as possible the last two weeks. He felt uncomfortable moving through an area so poorly lit, with so many angles someone could attack from. He wielded the sheers as a weapon in between cutting branches.

He gave a sigh of relief as he reached the opposite end of the Agrosim. He carefully set the sheers down in the same location he always did before entering the crew facilities. He had developed the habit of tracking the location of anything that could be used as a weapon. If his sheers had ever been moved he would have known immediately and known that he wasn't alone.

He made his way to the cafeteria. He had little interest in eating as he looked at the food that was readily available. He was going to have to start cooking before he lost all interest in eating. He grabbed an assortment of fruit, vegetables, and beans and sat down to eat.

Rick thought about the remaining work he had before he could enter the sleep chamber. All systems were showing proper levels and the ship had been thoroughly cleaned. He made sure to eat as much as he could. There was nothing more that he could think of. He rushed to consume his food as quickly as possible. The last two weeks had been in complete silence as he desperately listened for any noise from an intruder. Now that he was starting to build up confidence, he no longer wanted to be consumed with the loneliness of silence. He also thought the noise might help him stay present during his tasks so that time did not escape him so easily.

He promptly stood up and threw away his trash. Quickly he became anxious to escape his stress and loneliness in the sleep chamber. He was relieved, as he always was, to see the shears where he had left them as he entered the Agrosim. He took little time to do any work as he made his way through the room, and laid the sheers down next to the exit.

Bright light flooded through the door as Rick entered the crew quarters. The open space reminded him that he wasn't entirely over his fear yet. He walked as quickly toward his door as he could without making a noise. As he reached his door, he paused. His heart pounded in his chest loudly. He listened to it beat for a moment. He was tired of being awake, and knew he needed to be in the sleep chamber as much as possible to survive the trip. He was also scared of feeling lonely, and his loneliness had been getting worse the last couple of days. Yet despite his desires, he was afraid of the sleep chamber. It was getting harder for him to separate his dreams from reality, and he could never predict what his next dream would be. And what if there was someone on board that he hadn't found? He would be defenseless.

He turned around and walked to Matt's house. He turned on the lights as he entered the office. As he stood in front of Adelina's desk, he stared quietly at the portraits of his crew. Finally, he grabbed the photograph of Jessica and left the house.

He set the picture on the dresser in his room, which sat across from his sleep chamber. He did a final sweep of his room to make sure nothing was left out. He locked the handle to his bedroom door even though it could easily be picked or broken. He turned on the light in his bathroom before turning off the room lights, and then climbed into the sleep chamber. He felt comfortable knowing Jessica would be watching over him. He stared at her peacefully as oxygen poured into the sleep chamber. His eyes became heavy with drowsiness. As darkness began setting in he gazed at Jessica's face, a shadow shot across her image, and with that he fell asleep.

20 August 2340
Chapter 19

Rick opened the door to the sleep chamber. He looked at the clock. He had only slept for two weeks. There was no alarm. His chamber hadn't ejected him. He just woke up. He looked at the gauges. Their levels read normal. The room was pitch black, except for the soft light coming from the chamber's display. He normally leaves a light on, but it must have burned out, he thought.

He climbed out of the chamber and switched the light on. He turned to look at the portrait of his wife and noticed that it had been placed face down. He went to the bathroom to test the light. He always kept it on when he was in the sleep chamber. Flipping the switch, the light came on immediately. It had clearly been turned off. Rick walked out of the bathroom and felt grit between his toes. He bent over and saw dirt inside the carpet.

Whoever had been in his room had come from the garden. That had been Rick's fear. He never searched it thoroughly because he knew it was too dangerous should someone actually be in there. A single person could evade a dozen people searching for him in the garden anyway. If the person hid high enough then it would be above the cameras and they could consume food from the plants before they were harvested by the machines. The stats Rick had looked at before only showed a stable rate of consumption of the food that the machines had collected. Those stats didn't include food consumed directly from the plant.

Rick turned the lights off. He wasn't sure how he woke up, but regardless of whether it was intentional or not, he didn't want his intruder to know he was awake. He groped in the dark underneath his bed for an emergency kit. Inside the kit were night vision goggles that he quickly put on. His world turned to static white, green, and black. He turned his head quickly to scan his surroundings and the screen streaked white and green as it struggled to keep up with his movement. He would have to move slowly so the goggles could keep up.

He bent down to examine the carpet. After staring for a moment, he swore to himself. He wished he knew anything about hunting and tracks. He couldn't tell how old the track was or how large the person who left it was. He was confused as to how dirt could have stayed on someone's shoes this far away from the garden. He slowly followed the tracks out of his room and down the stairs. He fought the urge to scan his environment quickly. Each room he entered he searched slowly, knowing that he was at risk every time he first entered a new area.

Outside of his house was pure black. The lights did not turn on with his movement like they usually did. He walked quietly to an emergency light and saw broken glass. The light had been shattered. He could see in the distance that the door to the Agrosim was propped open. From where he stood he could not tell if the sheers were where he had left them, though he was sure they weren't. The open Agrosim loomed ominously before him. He lost all urge to follow the tracks. He wasn't sure why he had been allowed to safely pass through the Agrosim so many times before, but he knew he would not have that same luck this time. Instead, he turned and made his way to the cockpit.

The glow of computer lights emanated from the cockpit as he approached. He paused and watched the light come through the entry way, waiting for movement to signify the presence of the intruder. After several minutes passed he dared to venture forward. He carefully peaked around the corner into the cockpit. He could see no one. Several monitors were lit up with images from inside the ship. *The intruder had figured out how to view the security cameras,* thought Rick.

He moved farther into the cockpit to get a better look at the monitors. As he moved in he heard a *rip* and felt a sharp pain in his side. He looked down to see the point of a knife sticking out of his shirt. The knife had nearly missed him, and had only cut his flesh, but before he could react, his attacker had latched onto him from behind.

"Just give in and I won't kill you," whispered the man.

Rick struggled against the man's embrace.

"Stop!" The intruder demanded. "I don't want to have to kill you. Just show me how to run the ship."

"Why, so you can take it back to your colony? There's no hope for them, can't you see? If they can't get back to Earth then they are as good as dead," grunted Rick as he struggled.

"Are you kidding me? With Smith and his men dead, I have no home there. The colony would kill me if I ever returned. And why go back there? If I did, they would make me share the ship with everyone else. I just need you to show me how to run the ship."

"Why should I help you? You'll just kill me once you know what you need to know," replied Rick as he continued resisting.

"I'm going to get information out of you no matter what. If you play nice, I won't have to force it out of you."

As the man spoke, Rick could feel his grip loosen as he pulled the knife out of Rick's shirt. Rick threw his arm back, knocking the knife out of the man's hand. The man immediately tightened his hold on Rick and jammed his fingers into Rick's eyes. Rick screamed in pain as he kicked off a nearby surface, throwing the two men backwards. As they hit the wall behind them, the attacker let out a yell and Rick felt something sharp stab into his back. The man released his grip and Rick pushed away quickly.

The knife that Rick had knocked away now stuck out nearly an inch from the man's chest. The man appeared to be struggling to breathe. *The knife may have punctured his lung*, thought Rick. The man reached for Rick, his eyes filled with desperation. He attempted to speak, but he was unable to breathe in enough to do so. Drops of blood floated toward Rick as the man coughed while he struggled.

Rick turned his sight away from the man, refusing to look at him. He moved the man out of the cockpit and into the docking bay. He ignored the quiet pleas for help as he moved the man between the transition doors. The man floated helplessly as Rick reached the control panel to open the exterior bay door. Rick pressed a button and turned to see the man's terrified face as he realized what was happening. After several seconds the interior doors closed and Rick knew the exterior doors were opening.

He waited several minutes, absorbed in the silence around him. Finally, he closed the exterior doors. As the interior doors opened they revealed an empty space. He knew he was finally alone. As he looked at the empty area, he became overwhelmed with exhaustion and decided to resume his time in the sleep chamber.

He ignored the darkness as he made his way back to his room. The lights could be fixed later. He disregarded the open doors to the Agrosim, and entered his house. His body felt heavy as he climbed his stairs. As he entered the sleep chamber and closed the lid, he looked over to the bathroom. The light emitted was blurry as his eyes forced themselves to close. He was asleep before the chamber had a chance to take effect.

04 November 2340
Chapter 20

Rick squinted as his eyes struggled to adjust to the light cast from the bathroom. He turned his head and looked at the picture of Jessica that stood upright. He did not remember setting the picture up again before returning to the sleep chamber. He touched his side and did not feel a wound, though he thought it could have healed during the time he slept. He checked the clock. He had awakened on schedule.

He got out of the chamber and examined the carpet, which was completely clean. Rick's chest tightened as panic began overtaking him. He was beginning to think that his intruder had been a dream. If this was true, he thought, then he was no longer able to distinguish between his dreams and reality. A knot welled up in his stomach and he knew he had to immediately take action to gain as much control over the situation as possible.

Rick walked into his office and pulled out two notebooks from his desk. On the first he wrote "Dreams" and on the second "Awake." He wrote down everything he knew had happened, taking the time to write all the conversations he remembered having. He then wrote down his dreams and for each dream listed how he knew it was a dream. The easiest dreams were the ones in which he died. No explanation was needed. He decided to put his hallucinations into the awake notebook because they were events that could have an impact on him or his environment, and it was only a matter of interpretation of how those changes occurred.

His body calmed as he wrote. A sense of control returned to him. His panic was slowly replaced with sadness as he struggled to come to terms with the unfortunate circumstances he now lived with. He could no longer trust himself.

...

Rick's stomach grumbled loudly. He had spent several hours writing in his journals and had not yet eaten after waking from the sleep chamber. Despite knowing that he had been dreaming, he was still surprised to see the lights turn on as he exited his home. He walked casually through the crew quarters and into the Agrosim. He picked up the branch trimmers, but only bothered to trip branches that got in his way. He had become so exhausted from his weeks of paranoia before the sleep chamber, in combination with the stress of anticipating the sleep chamber itself, that he no longer had energy for fear. He did not worry about an attacker and did not constantly look over his shoulder as he had done before. He simply made his way to the cafeteria with complete calmness.

The cafeteria was fully stocked with the fruits and vegetables he had been consuming since the journey began. He no longer had an interest in eating unprepared food and decided that he would begin cooking actual meals. He grabbed the food he needed to settle his stomach and went into the kitchen to find the cookbooks.

The kitchen was large and open, with plenty of space to cook. It had sat clean and waiting for use ever since he had cleaned it up after Matt, now years ago. Thinking of the last time the kitchen had been used, Rick was shocked by how much time had gone by. Over two years had passed on the ship, and over forty years on Earth. Yet Rick had spent so much time in the sleep chamber that he hadn't had time to really cope with what had happened. His mind momentarily drifted as he thought about how strange it was that he had only been awake for a few weeks total since his crew had died yet they had been drifting in space for forty years. For a moment he wondered how much their bodies would have decayed in space and then forced himself to bring his attention back to what he was currently doing. He shook off the anxiety that was building within him and began hunting for a recipe he liked in the cookbooks.

...

Rick jumped off the treadmill and panted heavily. He paced around the large gym as his body settled into a rest. He turned off the TV that was playing a historical documentary. He had become fascinated with world history. Knowing that Earth was struggling for survival, yet he would never know what was happening, his imagination ran wild. He would often get lost in his thoughts, thinking of the inevitable dictators that would rise up, and the promises they would make. It also revived his sense of purpose, giving value to his mission, and served as a distraction from the reality of his situation.

He tried to imagine how the examples of world powers

he saw throughout history would translate to what was currently happening on Earth. Previous bouts of famine often revolved around droughts and collapsed economies. However, this was the first time that an entire world had to struggle with dwindling resources at the same time and know that the situation was not recoverable.

...

Rick turned away from the panel in core 'A' to look at his watch, which beeped quietly. The lasagna he was cooking was almost done. Over the past six weeks he had become very skilled in the kitchen and enjoyed cooking complicated meals. He was grateful for how time-consuming making the items for a meal from scratch was, though he always cooked enough for leftovers so he didn't have to cook every day.

He finished checking the core stats. He was about to enter the sleep chamber again, and was relieved to not have had any incidents with the ship or himself for the past six weeks. He had not had any paranoia or hallucinations, and his health had improved with his new diet and exercise. He paused and enjoyed the silence of the core room as he blankly stared at the black wall in front of him. He turned around to exit the room and noticed a wrench near the door that he didn't remember using. Without a second thought he picked it up, walked into the engineering room, and placed the wrench in a drawer.

As he made his way to the kitchen, excited for the meal he was about to eat, he reflected on the world history he had learned about recently. *How much are others having to struggle for food while I enjoy having access to a hundred times more food than I will ever need?* His waste was always recycled in a way that made the ship extremely efficient, but he wondered how much was wasted on Earth from hoarding or improper management and distribution.

03 January 2341
Chapter 21

"We are currently in a state of anarchy," said Elizabeth, a beautiful brunette in her early twenties. Her light brown eyes were lifeless as she spoke, resigned to her current state of existence. "After you killed Smith, several people tried to rise up and take his place. The people were encouraged by your actions and quickly killed Smith's successors before they had the chance to gain too much power or control. Unfortunately, this has scared potential leaders with the right intentions, those who could help, away from the position. People are doubtful of anyone being able to step up and lead with honesty and compassion."

"Did the conditions of the colony improve at all?" asked Rick.

"After Smith was gone, the masses rebelled against law enforcement and rooted out the bad eggs. With the rich no longer having someone to pay for protection crime skyrocketed for a while. We are all equally poor now," replied the woman.

"So no one has the courage to be a leader, and now everyone is equally miserable. Did my actions do any good?"

"A controlling leader is no worse than anarchy. The people are afraid, either of the leader or of each other. People who were rich have died from poverty, and those who would have died now have enough to live another day. In this world of extremes, there is no good or right answer. The only people who are happy are those who willingly choose to give of themselves to others. Unfortunately, those people are rare and require a disposition that comes from birth or painful revelation, neither of which can be forced. Though personally, I would rather live in fear because everyone has too many freedoms than the fear I lived with under oppression."

Rick shuffled forward slightly. He stood with Elizabeth in a line of people inside a crowded hallway. Her form was slender. Her clothing hung on her body loosely. She was clearly underfed. Their footsteps on the smooth, formerly white, metal flooring echoed off of the dingy gray metal walls. Looking out the window next to him, he could see Harper 9, the planet that the station orbited. The planet was completely covered in ice on its surface, which at times was hard to distinguish beneath the harsh storms that persisted year-round.

"Smith said before that it was criminals that were sent to work on Harper. Without any laws now, how do you decide who goes?" asked Rick.

"That was one of the easiest problems to solve, actually. We offer free food to the family of the person who goes. As long as they are working then their family has food. Should they die on the planet, then their family will receive one additional month of food. This offer has been so successful that we now have a waiting list of those who want to go."

"If everyone is fighting for themselves, how can anyone be guaranteed food?"

"The farmers are smart enough to know that it is easier to pay people to do the dangerous work on Harper than it is to actually do it themselves. They also know that as long as they give their food willingly, it won't be taken from them by force. As long as they give willingly, the people will protect them from individuals foolish enough to try and steal food. They also can make sure to keep enough for themselves this way."

"Well, I guess choice, or at least the illusion of choice, is better than force. What is Harper like?" asked Rick.

The two shuffled forward. Elizabeth stared out the window. Her stoic face was riddled with undercurrents of sadness. "If all we needed was water then it would be easy. Properly protected, an individual could last nearly an hour in the cold without freezing. The entire surface is ice, so water is not hard to find. But what we really need is the soil under the ice."

She moved forward in line, staring intently at the planet in the window. The view was almost entirely consumed by a planet that was nearly double the size of Earth. It's surface was nearly invisible underneath the wind and snow that engulfed its atmosphere.

"Our guess is that the planet used to be closer to its star. There is evidence of plants that used to grow for miles in the water until they reached the surface for sunlight. Unfortunately, the planet appears to have collided with Harper 7 at some point, which pushed the planet far enough away to freeze the surface. The collision also greatly deformed the surface of the planet, though you wouldn't be able to tell just from looking because the water on top keeps it looking round.

"The planet is so far away from the star it rotates around, that the water freezes down by nearly thirty meters. However, the planet is young, and still has a very active core.

so below that frozen ice is water, melted by the core, that sits on top of the land that we need. We have two domes under the ice right now that allow for people to grow crops and mine the land without water suits."

"Wow, that sounds dangerous," said Rick in awe.

"Yeah, we used to have three domes until a major earthquake crushed it. But as bad as it may sound, the dome is the safest place to be while on Harper. You might freeze to death on the surface, or get crushed in the tunnels to the dome, but most movement on Harper is minor enough to not put a dome at risk. If a tunnel closes because of ice movement, we can make a new one within a couple of hours."

The line moved forward. Rick looked around the crowd to see he was near the front, which turned through a door.

"Why are there tunnels and not just teleporters?" asked Rick.

"There are teleporters, but we only have ones capable of sending people and you have to get naked so the process is slow. The tunnels allow for large equipment and faster access to the surface if there is an emergency. It also allows for quicker transport of produce since we can transport much larger loads."

A young girl, around seven or eight with chaotic brown hair, ran up to Rick. Her clothes were filthy, ragged, and too short, despite her small size. "May I please have your spot in line, sir?" She asked sweetly.

Before he could speak Elizabeth responded. "You know, that is not allowed. If you two switch places then you will both be in trouble. Everyone gets their own turn."

Without warning, the girl kicked Elizabeth's leg and ran

off.

"What are we standing in line for anyway?" asked Rick.

"We're in line for food," replied Elizabeth.

"Oh, why can't I give that girl my spot? I'm not hungry," said Rick.

"Right now we need as many people as we can get to do work, whether it's working on Harper or trying to create new solutions for resources. That work takes energy and we can't afford to waste food on children. Most farmers will not give their food to kids."

"So the kids just starve to death?" asked Rick in shock.

"We decided that our best chance for survival was to nourish the strong, who are capable of working for more food and who might be able to find a solution," said Elizabeth calmly.

"But what if you don't find a solution, the amount one man could eat would feed three kids."

"Each life has a value. We've weighed our options and feel it is best to not keep them alive. It's no different than when you killed Smith."

"Of course it's different. Smith was a horrible person, but these kids have done nothing wrong. Yet you are going to let them die on the small chance that you can find a solution? Meanwhile, you eat well while they suffer."

"It's what you did to us."

14 February 2343

Chapter 22

Rick stepped off the scale. He had lost 13.6kg over the last two years. His large frame seemed to fit in the tight sleep chamber all too easily now. The desperation of Shadow Space Colony had haunted him the last few times he had used the sleep chamber. Ever since his first dream he had not been able to allow himself to eat more than what he needed to survive. Each bite was a reminder of the guilt he felt. Though, regardless of his feelings, he knew he needed to bring his weight up. He had not been physically prepared for the sleep chamber this last time, and it took nearly an hour to recover the strength in his legs enough to walk to the bathroom and weigh himself.

He had become deeply depressed. He had attempted to distract himself with the duties of the ship, but consistently felt empty and unfulfilled. Every time he looked into the mirror, a hollow, gaunt, despondent version of himself stared back at him. Logically, he knew his problem was simple. He had lost focus on the goal of the mission, resulting in him feeling that he lacked purpose or importance, thus allowing guilt for his previous actions to set in. The easiest way most people would counteract this situation would be through social affirmation from their peers. He did not have that luxury. Yet he knew that his survival and the success of his mission hinged upon his ability to control this issue.

With a sudden sense of what he needed to do Rick got

dressed and made his way out of his house. He entered Matt's house and walked into the office. He picked up the portrait of Matt, his chest proudly presented, hair slicked back and looking black with gel, and a toothy smile, and put it in his pocket.

. . .

Rick shook the pan as the vegetables sizzled, steam rose into the air, and a gust of aroma hit his nose.

"I don't know how much longer I can survive. I've been alone on this ship for over six years, awake for about six months of that, and until a couple years ago, I used my focus and determination for the mission as my strength. Now I have my doubts about my decisions and feel guilt over things I have done. I was able to distract myself with work in the past, but my guilt makes me feel lonelier than ever. My chest hurts each morning when I wake up and remember that I have no one." Rick stopped and looked at the picture of Matt that sat on the counter. "I'm sure you wouldn't know what that is like, you were always popular."

Rick picked up Matt's picture and carried it to the dining area.

"I hate being awake. Yet it is my dreams that torment me. My biggest fear is that one day my dreams will fill in all the gaps that currently let me know they never happened. I'm doing what I can to avoid the inevitable, but I think I got started after too much damage had been done. Staying mentally healthy was going to be difficult with a full crew. It's impossible by myself."

Rick ate his food quickly. He had recovered some of his

lost weight over the past three days since he started talking to Matt's photo. He also had the energy to perform some of the ship maintenance that he had let go of the last couple of times he had been awake.

"I went over the numbers in my head earlier," said Rick. "When we left, I had a twenty-five percent chance of living until the very end of the mission. With everyone gone, from a purely physical perspective, my chances dropped to probably twelve percent. I think that if I take care of myself I might be able to last another year of being awake before I'm completely insane. If we're lucky, I won't immediately kill myself. I've considered figuring out my chances of survival beyond that point, but there is no way for me to know what kind of lunatic I'll be. Sort of like how people don't know what kind of a drunk they are until after their first time. I assume this will be like that, though less puking. I hope."

Rick finished eating and disposed of his dirty dishes. He picked up Matt's image, with Matt's boisterous smile that always greeted him, and made his way out of the cafeteria.

"What I find most interesting is how much time I spend being afraid of going insane. The funny part being that once I am actually insane I won't even know it, because if I were aware enough to put the pieces together then I probably wouldn't actually be insane yet."

He walked into the gym and set the picture down on a table. "My goal is to make a list of the things I experience that are not possible to have happened. If anything happens that is on the list then I know it isn't real. I will also have a record of past dreams or hallucinations that I can study and find patterns in. This way, if something technically possible happens, but it strictly follows a pattern of something I know didn't happen, then I will have reason to doubt and investigate my current experience."

He jumped on a treadmill and began jogging. "This, of course, is contingent upon my willingness to do the work, and there is no guarantee of how I will act when this stuff comes to pass."

"I also find it ironic that I have to act insane to hopefully stave off actually going insane. I can't just talk to myself like a normal person would do when they are alone. I have to talk to objects. However, I have to talk to them as though they are not objects but real people. This is, of course, to trick my mind into thinking it is getting the things it needs. I have to outsmart my own mind, all while knowing I'm doing it. It reminds me of a joke. 'I was sitting around thinking about how my brain is the most amazing part of my body until I suddenly remembered where those thoughts came from.' It's like that, but in reverse."

Rick stepped on the sides of his treadmill to take a breath. He looked at Matt. "I also wonder if I'm going to go insane thinking about how I need to find ways to not go insane. In all seriousness, though, my efforts do seem to be having a positive impact. All of this exercise has gotten my sleeping schedule back to roughly a 25 hour day and night cycle and I seem to be a little faster at daily tasks. I still see lights in my peripheral vision on occasion, though I did have my eyesight checked and everything was normal. Haven't figured out what that is about."

...

Adelina's picture sat on the edge of a garden box next to

where Rick was working to trim branches. It had a playfully seductive pose that had been taken by Matt after multiple failed attempts for "being too boring," he had claimed, at her birthday party. Over the past two weeks he had incorporated each of the crew members' pictures into his routine.

"Do you think there is any risk that the machines could be overwhelmed and possibly damaged by the excess branches from me staying in the sleep chamber longer than we ever planned for?" Asked Rick as he looked over his shoulder at Adelina. "I'm not sure if they will always clear their own paths properly and I have nothing to worry about or if I just so happen to have been very lucky until now."

Rick set his branch trimmers down and sat next to Adelina's picture, her joyous laugh unconcerned with his labor, as he wiped away the sweat around his eyes.

"I guess the only way to know is to wait and see what happens. I don't really have a choice about staying longer in the sleep chamber. It's the safest way to make sure I stay healthy until the end of the trip. I feel more confident about the rest of the ship after talking it through with Jason, but this is the one spot where nature still has a say in how things play out."

Rick looked at Adelina's picture and sighed. "I guess in me too."

06 August 2367
Chapter 23

Rick ate leftover vegetable stew for dinner quietly. He had grown fond of listening to the wild imaginings of an ancient society. Tonight, Michael Crichton's *Timeline* was being read over the speakers. When he woke up this morning, he couldn't find any of his pictures. He did occasionally forget them in random places if he became distracted, so he wasn't too concerned about it. The story over the intercom served as a good distraction while he waited to find them.

"The crowd screamed and pounded the railings like a drumbeat."

Being read to did often fulfill his need to be spoken to. It was, of course, a one-sided conversation, but it kept away the feeling of isolation that he felt, especially whenever he misplaced the images of his crew.

As Rick listened he noticed that the audio was gradually getting quieter. Suddenly the audio turned off completely. The unexpected silence filled with malice and anticipation. Rick stood up and whipped around quickly. He looked for movement, anything to indicate a hallucination. He touched his back pocket and felt his notebook. He kept his notebook with him at all times. He often felt great fatigue after a hallucination, and if he waited until after he slept to write it down, then he wouldn't be able to tell if he had dreamed about a hallucination or actually had one.

Rick held his breath and listened. He heard faint noises

coming from the kitchen. He approached the kitchen cautiously. The noises remained faint. They sounded to him like light footsteps. As Rick reached the door to the kitchen, he could hear the walk-in freezer door open and close. He lingered as he thought about what he should do next, unsure of what he could do to protect himself if he moved forward.

He entered the kitchen anxiously. The room was dimly lit by emergency lighting. A staleness overpowered the space that made the room feel foreign to him. A dull thud came from within the freezer. Rick's heart beat in his chest furiously. When he reached the freezer, he paused. He debated if he should lock the door or look inside as his hand waited above the door handle with trepidation.

His curiosity eventually got the better of him and he slowly turned the door handle. He heard the click as the door unlatched. The door swung open, explosively, knocking Rick to the floor. A cloud of thick white fog poured out of the freezer. He could see shadows moving within the rolling cloud of moisture, several masses that looked like human figures except that they moved fluidly, intertwining with each other.

"Join us," said a collection of voices in a raspy, hateful whisper.

Rick froze in fear. The shadows approached, slowly, dancing in and out of each other in a hypnotic fashion. One shadow broke from the group and moved closer to Rick, emerging from the fog as it reached out toward him, a purple and black hand with broken and peeling skin covered in ice. His shock was shattered as he became consumed with a new level of horror. He instantly jumped to his feet and began running out of the kitchen. His hands groped the counters and walls for purchase to help propel himself forward.

The fog gushed out of the freezer, moving quickly toward Rick. He slammed the door to the kitchen and continued running. Looking over his shoulder as he ran, he saw smoke seeping through the cracks of the door until it shot open. The smoke bellowed and churned as it raced toward him.

As he ran toward the Agrosim he saw a red light coming from the teleporter next to the door. Not wanting to waste time figuring out why it wasn't active, he ran into the Agrosim. Branches slashed at his arms and face as he made his way through the room. As he neared the end of the room, he saw the teleporter near the door had a green light. Rick approached the teleporter and slammed on the keys to call up his house's teleporter. Looking behind him he could barely see through the fog that was now less than thirty meters away. The teleporter chimed, signaling that it was ready. Rick jumped in and it sent him away just as the fog threatened to consume him.

He was now near the entrance, just inside his house, and he was engulfed in fog. He disabled the teleporter as he stepped out and stretched out his arms as he blindly moved through the imposing white mass. Anxiously, he moved forward until his foot kicked the first step of his stairs. He dropped onto his hands and scrambled up the stairs on all four as quickly as he could.

As he reached his room, he heard the front door bang open. From downstairs he could just make out the repulsive whispers of his pursuers. Rick wanted to hide inside the closet, but knew it would be impossible to keep them out. Instead he climbed into his sleep chamber and closed the door. He slammed on the controls to activate hibernation mode, which is the only way to lock the door.

The shadowy figures emerged from the doorway and moved toward Rick. He heard the click of the door locking and panicked. He only had a brief moment to write in his journal before he fell asleep. He reached for his pocket and grabbed his journal as hands suddenly streaked across the glass door. Furiously, he began writing, his hands shaking as they scribbled content in a panicked frenzy. He held his breath to slow down the sleep chamber's effects. As he wrote, the hands that desperately groped the door began to lighten and fade away. Despite his efforts, his thoughts became cloudy. As his eye lids became too heavy to stay open, he looked around. All the fog was gone. Then it was replaced with black.

24 August 2367
Chapter 24

"I looked through all the pages," said Rick as he paced back and forth in the kitchen. "Yes, I even looked through previous entries to see if I accidentally wrote on top of them. The truth is that, despite what I think, the facts say, it was only a dream."

Rick paused and stared at the picture of Jason that sat on the counter. Jason's dark eyes were giving him a smoldering look that came all too naturally to him.

"Jason, I've already gone over this. Everything was in order when I entered the kitchen, even though I remember knocking things over. There also is nothing about it in the journal, so it never happened."

He looked around the kitchen for anything that could be out of place.

"The journal is accurate!" exploded Rick. "You are never to doubt the journal again. The system works. If it is in the journal, then it happened. The second we question the journal is the moment that I have lost all hope of keeping my mind under control."

He continued to pace quickly. "On a lighter note, Jason, I've decided to forgive you." Rick paused and looked at the picture of Jason. "You knew that we had to stick to a schedule so the engines wouldn't cool down too much, yet you proposed a plan that would either take too long and force the engines to cool off and risk damage when starting them up again, or compromise on the safety of the crew by breaking protocol and having the entire crew leave the ship."

Rick sighed, "I'll admit that it was my call to follow your plan or not, so I am partly to blame, but it never would have happened had you just been content with what we had."

Rick's watch chimed quietly. He looked at it briefly. "Sorry Jason, five 'o clock, I've got a date."

. . .

Rick gazed out at the field of grass that stretched endlessly before him. He watched the blades of grass bend gracefully back and forth to the movement of the wind. The sun was slowly setting, painting the sky pink and orange.

"No matter how amazing the view is, you are the most beautiful thing I've ever seen," said Rick as he turned and looked at the picture of Jessica that sat next to him, her eyes seeming to meet his. He lay on his back on a blanket he had placed in the simulation room. He allowed himself to ignore the hard floor he was on and just enjoy the scenery. "We just never had enough time together, you know?" He sighed. "Everything we did revolved around school or training. We never had a chance to get away. I wanted to be here with you, but being here alone makes me jealous that you aren't stuck on this ship. Yet, despite my jealousy, I'm consumed with this need to complete my mission, no matter how badly I wish I was with you."

He stared up at the sky, the colorful clouds above him moving slowly. "When I am with the others, I am gone ninety percent of the time. I become lost in the idea that I am actually with them. I never have that with you. You always bring me home. No matter how hard I try, you always gave me more than I can imagine. Being with you was so amazing that it is impossible to remember how truly great it was. All I know is that I've never felt that since you've been gone, and I never will. This truth, above all other things, will keep me grounded. You will always bring me home."

...

Rick sat peacefully in the cockpit and watched the screens in front of him. Every two minutes the display updated with a new image of the stars outside the ship. He thought about the data that the ship had collected over the years and wondered if there was still anyone who would care about it. He rarely thought about what might be happening on Earth anymore. It would be years before he would stop the ship again to open communication, and he doubted he would be contacted by anyone when that time came. He looked around. Each member of his crew sat at their designated spot.

Rick let out a sigh. "Sometimes I think I allow situations to stress me out," he said to no one in particular. "Sitting here, watching the universe pass by, helps put everything into perspective. The Earth is less than dust in this universe and I am just a spec from that dust. The universe existed for billions of years before man existed. It doesn't care if a spec, moving too fast to be seen or detected by anyone, makes it to a planet to save a bunch of people that likely no longer exist."

Rick let out another sigh. "No, Taisha, I don't think that is destructive thinking. I'm not using it as an excuse to quit, just to make it feel like the weight of the universe isn't on my shoulders."

Rick paused.

"You're right, Matt. I just need to do whatever it takes to survive. My chance of survival is around one percent now. I'm assuming it will be impossible for me to succeed, which is great. There is no pressure when failure is assumed, only a pleasant surprise if success is achieved."

Rick paused again.

"Taisha, your doubt is not constructive in any manner, and I demand you remain quiet until you can be more positive in your thinking. Psychoanalyzing every little thought that comes into my head isn't needed right now. My thinking isn't putting me or the mission at risk. I'm still motivated to try, and it doesn't negatively impact my mood. If I wanted to negatively impact my mood I would just think about the struggles that are happening on Earth and the people I can't save even if I am successful."

14 April 2412
Chapter 25

"When the light passes by us again, that is when we will make a run for it," said Jason. "And when we get to the grass, make sure to be careful. They've hidden bear traps in there that are hard to see because of how tall the grass is. Any questions?" His face was stern, though the dark of night and the camouflage he wore made him hard to see clearly.

Jessica, Tim, Linda, Taisha, Matt, and Adelina all shook their heads. They were huddled inside a deep ditch to the side of a road looking at a section of farm land in the distance. The group wore matching dark brown jumpsuits to conceal themselves. Rick peeked over the top of the mound they were hiding behind. The security guarding the farm was tight. First, they needed to pass through the open dirt that was patrolled by spot lights from atop a tower in the corner of the property. Each corner of the farm had a spotlight that would cycle back and forth. Once they passed the open dirt, they would reach waist high grass that they could attempt to hide behind.

Still in the ditch, the group waited as the light passed by slowly. Each person shifted anxiously for their moment of action. As the light passed them, the group immediately jumped up and began running toward the grass ahead of them. Before entering the grass they laid down, hidden behind the grass, but not on top of it, so that they didn't dent it and give away their location.

"We are at a disadvantage. If it were windy right now, we might be able to sneak through the grass, hidden by its natural movement. As it is right now, any movement in the grass will be obvious and get us caught, regardless of any disguises," said Jason.

"We'll have to go to plan B and create a distraction," said Matt as he handed Molotov cocktails to Taisha, Linda, and Adelina. "You know the plan," he said to them. "Move around the farm clockwise from here. One of you at each corner. Linda will go to the last corner and be the first to throw her cocktail. Then you two will throw yours once you see the first one go."

"Guys, there has to be some other way to get in there, this is a horrible idea," interjected Rick. "If we burn the place down, we can never come back for more food."

"We are just setting up a distraction. The fires will be far enough away to not actually threaten the crops, assuming they leave their posts to stop the fires," responded Matt, his large mass struggling to remain hidden.

"Burning the crops would actually produce a higher yield the next growth season, so it wouldn't be the end of the world," added Adelina.

The light passed by them as they hid behind a wall of grass. Linda got on her knees and began making her way around the farm. Taisha and Adelina following a short distance behind. The rest of the group stayed where they were, waiting for the signals to tell them they could move forward.

"Honestly, Rick, who cares if this entire farm burns down anyway?" said Tim angrily. "We know they have been burning down the crops of any farmers that don't want to follow their price increases. They are specifically trying to make people indebted to them so that they can take land away from those who need food."

"The Richardson farm sold its food at the lowest prices they could, often giving it away to anyone who could do an honest day's work. They all died in the fire that consumed their farm and it was started by these guys," said Tim.

"I know what you're thinking, Rick. 'Two wrongs don't make a right.' However, that assumes that this is wrong. They killed people who didn't want to steal from the poor and the starving. This is simply justice," said Jason.

"But you said we are just making a distraction. We aren't actually destroying their crops, right?" asked Rick.

"Of course not. That would be wasteful," replied Matt.

Before Rick had a chance to question Jason further, a siren rang loudly as smoke began to rise into the air. Rick peeked over the grass and could see flames spreading across the grass in the northeast corner of the farm. He looked to his left and saw the flames exploding in response to Adelina's fire.

"All available personnel are needed to fight fires at the Northwest, Southwest, and Northeast corners of the farm," announced the speakers surrounding the farm.

Jason signaled for everyone to wait. The patrolling guards ran to the nearest fire and the spotlights were focused on the area surrounding the action.

When their surroundings were clear, Jason signaled for everyone to move forward quickly. As they ran Matt distributed wire cutters to everyone. They were able to breach the fence protecting the farm quickly, without being noticed. Jason entered first and helped the others get through the fence.

"You guys go gather as much food as you can and make sure not to get caught. I'll meet you guys with Linda, Taisha, and Adelina a half mile east from the Southeast corner of the farm," said Jason as he ran off with two Molotov cocktails.

"What is he doing?" asked Rick.

"We don't have time for questions. We have to hurry," said Jessica as she grabbed Rick's arm and ran for cover in the corn field. She wore a gray beanie to conceal her long fiery hair.

They quickly grabbed corn as they ran through the field.

"Don't bother too much with this stuff. It's the tomatoes and bell peppers that are the healthiest on a limited diet. Too bad this farm doesn't have nuts, that would be the best," said Jessica.

As they gathered fruits and vegetables, while the guards were distracted by fires, a new alarm rang over the intercom.

"Fire has spread to the northeast corner of the house, near the armory."

Rick turned and looked at the house just in time to see a series of explosions. The ammunition had caught fire and created an explosion that completely leveled the house, sending debris hundreds of meters into the air. He quickly jumped on top of Jessica to shield her from the debris that crashed around them.

Guards from all over the farm abandoned their posts to assist in the fire at the house. Rick hid behind plants and waited for everyone to go by. The rest of the group continued filling their bags with produce.

When the coast was clear and the guards were obviously

distracted by the fires, the group exited the farm. Once they were a safe distance from the farm, they ran as quickly as they could to meet with the rest of their group. Jason was the first that Rick saw, serving as a look out for the rest of the group that had already arrived.

"How could you do that, Jason? You killed anyone in or even near that house," accused Rick.

"You can try to shift responsibility by being a neutral party all you want, but the simple fact is that everyone has to choose sides. They chose their side when they killed innocent people for the sake of making more money and having more control. They were due some punishment, and if it hadn't come from us, it would have come from someone else. Like it or not, we are a part of this world and its problems. You can pretend as though you are above getting involved, but you were there with us, stealing food," replied Jason.

"You should have at least been responsible about it. Because of the fire you started, there is no way the crops won't be burned to the ground."

"The amount of damage they could have done with the ammunition I destroyed far exceeds the crops they lost. And I didn't really have the option to do things carefully. They were already on high alert. I had to get in and out as quickly as possible."

"Rick," said Jessica gently. "You can't save everyone, and you know this. All we can do now is move forward. You can't let your doubts about previous decisions cloud your current actions. What's right isn't always right and what's wrong isn't always wrong, but what's done is done, so just let it be."

07 February 2485
Chapter 26

"Believe it or not, Jason, we've made the halfway point," said Rick quietly. "I've done everything I could to avoid stopping the ship. I've checked all ship vitals consistently to make sure no damage to the ship went unnoticed. But, despite my best efforts, it's regulation to make a stop and do maintenance on the ship."

He moved around the cockpit, gracefully, checking the monitors around him.

"We've been lucky. All this time and only two plates need repair. The work can easily be done by one person and shouldn't take more than two hours."

A chime rang over the intercom. "One hour remaining until complete deceleration achieved." Announced a female voice.

"Considering how well the ship has done so far, I think I could forgo general maintenance of the ship's externals after today. I have to weigh my odds and take risks wisely. By the time the ship will need maintenance again, I will be too old. It will be safer to not stop and risk the ship than to stop and risk myself." He took great comfort in knowing this would be the only time he would have to do this.

He pushed on the chair in front of him and quickly shot out of the cockpit and into the docking bay.

"Hey Tim, how's the shuttle doin'?" asked Rick. He examined the shuttle almost every day for the past two weeks in preparation for this event. He found himself in the docking bay so often that he stopped taking Tim's photo with him when he left. Tim wore a Hawaiian shirt with the top three buttons undone. The collar flared out to show his pecks as much as possible. "I know, I know, I'm always in here and nothing has changed, but this will be my last time checking the shuttle."

He moved over to the table where his tools were laid out. As the ship had changed temperature through travel, some of the plates had lost the precise shape and heat flow that they needed. The adjustments were simple enough that Rick could do them alone. He would put a machine with a tension sensor on the warped plate that could measure tension across the plate and loosen the bolts that held the plate down according to what the tuner said so that the tension would shift and the plate would regain the necessary shape.

Each tool that needed to, turned on properly. Everything was in perfect working order and had a full charge on power supplies. Rick took his time carefully loading each one onto the shuttle and arranged them for quick and easy access. The time passed rapidly as he worked, and a chime rang over the intercom signaling that the hour until the ship stopped had passed. The ship was at full rest.

Rick was fully suited up for the mission and only had to put his helmet on before entering the shuttle. He made sure the seal was tight and air pressure in the suit was optimal and then opened the bay doors so the shuttle could exit the ship.

Buzzers rang and lights flashed as the first door opened and Rick moved the shuttle forward. As the door came to a close behind him, his breathing became more rapid and he grew short of breath. The door opening in front of him made his heart pound loudly in his chest. The darkness that had consumed his crew, the same one that he had drifted through when he almost lost his ship at Shadow Space Colony, sprawled out endlessly before him. Rick was no longer deceived by the hateful expanse that tricked its viewer into perceiving itself as the epitome of loneliness. He saw it for what it was, a vengeful void, enraged that life excluded it, living safely inside its cocoon. So lustful for life was the void, that the second it had a life within its grasp, it would tear it to pieces robbing it of its essence.

He moved the shuttle forward, out into the black ocean. The shuttle moved peacefully and the gauges on board had normal readings. Rick felt a wave of relief that, despite how long ago he had made his repairs to the shuttle, everything still worked properly. Numbers and arrows danced on the windshield as the shuttle labeled the panels of the ship, allowing him to know where he needed to go. As he reached the end of the ship a panel became outlined in red on the windshield. He peered out at the panel and read the number "192816," which was consistent with the computer.

He stopped the shuttle and opened the door. Floating out, he quickly anchored the shuttle to the ship and retrieved his tools. The tuner for the panel reminded him of the collapsed frame for a large umbrella. As he opened the tuner, like a menacing claw, when the arms extended outward, he attached each arm to a bolt on the edge of the panel. At the center of these arms was a short column that came to rest gently at the center of the panel. He turned the device on with a switch on the center column, and it flashed a warning to not touch the panel. It then emitted a low frequency vibration that it used to "play" the panel and test how the tension was currently distributed. The screen on the tuner showed a progress bar as the arms gradually tightened or loosened the bolts they were attached to.

The process of tuning took about 30 minutes, though Rick had not realized how much time had passed as he watched patiently. Finally, the screen on the tuner flashed green and Rick detached it from the panel. He quickly loaded it onto the shuttle and began making his way to the second panel.

The lights on the window once again danced as it labeled the panels. He was nearing the end of the ship. As he approached, the ship's edge looked like the crest of a water fall, turning a corner that he could not see around and pouring into the infinite black void before him. Red appeared on the glass as the next panel for maintenance approached. He brought the shuttle to a stop and began unloading the tuner. He moved as fast as he could. Being so close to the end of the ship gave him a fear he had not expected.

He attached the tuner and activated it with haste. The screen flashed and a progress bar appeared as it began emitting a low vibration. Rick's heart began beating faster. He quickly checked the levels on his suit. Everything was normal. The progress bar on the tuner crawled forward painfully slow.

With anxiety Rick looked at the end of the ship, sixty meters away. He appreciated the perfectly smooth, predictable horizon that it created against the chaotic, uncontrollable universe that served as its backdrop. The ship was white with a semi-reflective cover which allowed it to reflect the maximum amount of heat as it occasionally passed nearby stars. Rick found comfort in analyzing the ship, his shield from the unknown.

Rick noticed a green flashing from the side of his helmet. He turned to the tuner which had completed its task. He switched it off and began collapsing it. He was relieved to be done and hopeful that he would never have to leave the ship again. Closing the rear hatch of the shuttle after loading the tuner, he took one last look at the horizon of the ship. His eyes traced along the perfectly smooth arch of the ship. As his eyes followed the line, he noticed an anomaly.

It looked like a chip in one of the panels. He squinted to see from far away. As he struggled to see, he fired his suit thrusters to move slowly closer. About ten meters closer, he realized that it was not a chip in the panel, but something black on top of it. *At the speed the ship travels, nothing should be able to attach itself to the ship*, he thought.

He turned to look at the shuttle. He had traveled about half way to the edge of the ship. *This is not right*, he thought. He quickly came to a stop. He returned his attention back to the edge of the ship, struggling to discern what he was seeing. The object moved to the right and slowly another dark spot appeared to the left of it. Rick gasped and fumbled with the controls for his suit's thrusters. They fired a short burst that sent him slowly moving backwards toward the shuttle. He was frozen with fear, unable to realize that holding the thruster trigger down didn't make them fire continuously. They only worked in short bursts and had to be triggered each time.

The object grew longer as it moved down the ship, closer toward Rick. As he drifted backward, he watched intently.

The left object lifted off of the ship slightly and moved closer until it gently touched the ship again.

A mass began to appear between the two objects and Rick realized he was looking at arms crawling over from the end of the ship and the head was starting to show. It looked like a burnt corpse. Its movements were stilted and startling.

"I'm hallucinating," whispered Rick to himself.

He stared intently as eyes appeared. Even from a distance he could see they were blood red. The corpse came fully into view, slowly crawling toward Rick. Long crispy hair extended from its head in patchy chunks.

"You're not her," said Rick in a whimper. "You're not Jessica." He remained petrified with fear, unable to realize why he wasn't moving away faster.

The corpse gradually gained speed. Her head rotated around in sharp, jerking movements. It rotated until her mouth was where her forehead should have been. Methodically the mouth opened and closed. A five inch tongue that came to a sharp point shot out when her mouth opened, flicking around in all directions. Her hands and chest left black smudges on the ship's surface as she slithered forward.

As she picked up speed, she began to gallop on all four until she leaped toward Rick. He was unable to prevent the full body embrace as she latched onto him. She dug her fingers into his sides and squeezed him until it forced the air out of his lungs. The suit was made with a fabric that was designed to prevent small punctures which stopped her fingers from tearing holes into his suit. She bit at his face violently, but was unable to break the glass that shielded him. Her frustration mounted as she realized she could not directly injure him, though she still embraced him so tightly that he could not breathe.

Finally, in her frustration, she began banging her head into his helmet as hard as she could. After the first two blows, she paused for a moment to examine the damage. She immediately saw that no damage was done and repeated banging her head with increased enmity, no longer pausing.

Rick watched helplessly, still unable to breathe, as her head began to crack open. Just as he noticed blood and matter beginning to pour from her skull, he passed out.

. . .

Rick woke to the sound of gentle beeping. As his eyes opened he could see the shuttle a hundred meters away. Realizing where he was, he quickly looked around for any sign of Jessica. There was no sign of her, and his suit appeared to be without damage. He noticed the noise in his suit again as it changed from a beep to a constant drone. His suit had thirty minutes of oxygen left.

Firing his thrusters a couple times, he swiftly made his way back to the shuttle. Upon starting up the shuttle, the displays came to life and the plate he had re-calibrated was outlined in green. He made his way back to the docking bay as fast as he could. He was unsure of how long the ship had been at rest, but didn't want to waste another moment.

As soon as the docking bay doors were closed and the shuttle was parked he jumped out of the shuttle and made his way to the cockpit. He removed his space suit while the ship began its launch sequence. With the ship beginning to accelerate, he reached for the journal he kept in his back pocket. With shaking hands, he began writing about the hallucination he had just had.

30 January 2501
Chapter 27

Rick idly chopped the branches in the Agrosim. He wiped the sweat from his forehead and turned to look at the picture of Tim that sat next to him on the ground. Tim's eyes, a blue that was accentuated by the Hawaiian shirt he wore, greeted Rick happily. "I knew that a lifetime in outer space would get boring over time with just the eight of us out here, but it sure doesn't help with you just sitting there quietly."

"Yes, yes. I know. You try your hardest. I believe you." Rick grunted as he worked his way through an exceptionally thick branch.

"The funny thing is that, I enjoy complaining about boredom, but the only exciting things that happen are horrible dreams and hallucinations. What can possibly happen to me that is different from normal daily life and isn't also an emergency? Despite my complaining, I'm actually terrified of anything abnormal happening."

Rick set down his tools and wiped the sweat from his brow. He examined his hands, which had grown hard and callused over the years. They were no longer slim and youthful, but thick and worn.

He looked at Tim as he caught his breath. "I think I've had all I can take for now. Do you want to stay here and keep working?"

Rick paused.

"Okay. Have fun."

Rick left Tim's picture where it was and made his way to the kitchen. He waved to the pictures of Taisha and Jason as he passed them. Entering the kitchen, Linda's photo was there waiting for him. She wore an elegant, black cocktail dress with her hair pinned up in a way that made it fan outward behind her head.

"I have no idea what I'm going to make Linda," said Rick with mild agitation. "I just got done cutting the branches that you refuse to help out with, so I'll just have to figure it out now that I'm in here."

Rick opened the refrigerator and began thinking about what looked tastiest to him.

"Alright, I'm sorry. I was a little snappy because I'm tired. I didn't mean to take it out on you. What sounds good to you?"

He turned to look at Linda's picture. She had a smile that rose on one side more than the other, which gave her expression a thoughtfulness and warmth that Rick appreciated.

"You're on as much of an Asian food kick as I am, I guess. Doesn't hurt that it's so fun to make and keeps me busy for a long time. Alright, we can do kung pao tonight, but right now it's time for breakfast, not dinner."

Rick turned back to the open refrigerator. He let out a sigh, pulled out a bowl with batter in it, and closed the refrigerator. "I guess I'll do waffles since I have left over mix from yesterday."

"I've got to stop falling back on these tried-and-true recipes and branch out some more," he said as he poured the mix into the waffle iron. "I've learned several different dinners, but I'm usually too tired in the morning to think about trying something new. That being said, I'm really getting tired of the same thing every morning. Maybe later today I'll try making some muffins."

The waffle iron chimed when ready. Rick slid the waffle onto his plate, drenched it in syrup, and then carried his plate along with the picture of Linda to the eating area. Taisha and Jason were waiting for him.

"Good morning guys." The three photos were arranged around the table at different seats, all facing Rick.

He looked at Taisha. She wore a red v-neck sequin dress that highlighted her slender yet elegant shape and dark skin.

"No, I'm fine, just a little tired. Today is shaping up to be just like any other."

He took a bite of his food.

"I know, I know. I've been trying to stay mentally active, I promise."

Rick reached into his back pocket and grabbed a sketch pad that he kept next to his hallucination journal and slapped it onto the table.

"See? I've taken up drawing lately. Combined with writing poetry, playing guitar, reading, carving wood from the branches I cut down, and tinkering with all the electronics we have around here, my day is totally full." Rick smiled at her in a way that asked for approval.

"Yes, I know I'm getting old. I'm also getting plenty of exercise and rest too."

Rick finished his meal and stood up. "I feel like I've had this conversation a thousand times, and while it's fun every time I have to make my rounds checking the ship. You guys enjoy yourselves."

Rick returned his dish to the kitchen and quickly cleaned

it before teleporting to the cockpit.

Rick looked around as he made his way to his seat. The majority of the cockpit looked as new as the day he arrived on the ship since it had barely been used. He strapped himself in so he didn't have to constantly keep himself from floating away and then began pressing buttons on the console in front of him. In a routine that had been ingrained into him throughout the years, he made the screen in front of him flow through many gauges and measurements. His vision went half-blurred as he just looked for anything that was different. Everything he saw had green in it.

Same as always, thought Rick.

Thirty minutes later and Rick had reviewed everything related to the basic functioning of the ship. He knew there was a great chance that he was wasting his time, that the ship would alert him if anything was wrong. However, the emergency system was tested in such short and specific scenarios that in Rick's mind it was in large part untested. Of course, he would never know if emergency systems didn't work properly unless he looked for it.

After he was done he made his way to the lab and reviewed the most recent samples of the vegetation and soil before making his way back to the kitchen for lunch.

Rick sniffed the bread he had made several days earlier as he also gave it a gentle squeeze. Still fresh. All of the ingredients for a sandwich were in the front of the refrigerator since he often made meals in bulk and then had the same meal several days in a row. He threw together a sandwich as he distracted himself, thinking about what he wanted to draw in his sketchpad next. He then made his way out to the table where the photos of Linda, Taisha, and

Jason had remained since breakfast.

Rick let out a sigh before biting into his tuna sandwich. "I know it's easier to make a lot of food at once and then not worry about the effort or even thinking about what to eat for a few days, but the repetition is killing me."

Rick looked at the photo of Jason. Rick interpreted Jason's smoldering look as disdain for Rick's monotonous food.

"I know, right? As if my day isn't repetitive enough as it is, then I do this to myself. Speaking of things being the same as always; everything with the ship is completely normal."

Rick ate in silence for a moment before turning to Taisha. "I know this may upset you as the local art historian, but I think I'm going to take an unpopular stance and say that after reading up on some painters I am very unimpressed by Jackson Pollock."

He paused and waited for Taisha. Her large smile that showed her bright white teeth framed in an electric red lipstick served as her response.

"Oh, good. I'm glad you agree. I was just trying to find some inspiration for things to draw and then I got off on this tangent of famous painters, and I can't honestly say that I think what he did was painting. Dripping or throwing household paint on a canvas doesn't require any technique. It sounds more like a disgruntled housewife. It's something that anyone can copy. I could understand putting it on top of or inside of another painting so that it could convey the emotions of the underlying or surrounding painting, but, as it is, I'm just thoroughly unimpressed."

Rick finished his sandwich, leaned back in his seat, and

let out a low groan as he stretched.

"Well, I'm off to practice my guitar before I hit the gym and finish up my daily gardening. I'll meet you guys back here for dinner. Don't get into any trouble while I'm gone."

...

With eager relief to be done Rick finished his last set in the gym. For the sake of being as fit as possible when waking up from the sleep chamber he knew he needed as much muscle mass as possible. But each set had become a chore for him that yielded no emotional reward. He set down his weights and with complete indifference walked past the mirror without looking. He teleported his towel home and then walked to the kitchen, grabbing the photo of Jason along the way.

Carefully, he set Jason on the counter and began making dinner. He was comfortable with the recipe he was working on, so he talked as he went.

"I'm about to go back into the sleep chamber." Rick glanced at Jason. "I'm trying to keep a positive outlook on things, but I'm stuck in this cycle of hell where I can't decide what aspect of my life to look forward to or to dread. Part of me is happy to be in the sleep chamber because at least then there is nothing expected of me. My health is generally stable and my sanity is impacted a little bit by the dreams I have, I'm sure, since they are so vivid, but it can't be worse than when I am awake. And to that point, unlike with dreams, I have a very real possibility of getting hurt when I am hallucinating. At the same time though, I hate going in there because I feel like my life is wasting away."

Rick looked at Jason.

"Yeah, I get it. I'm not exactly going to have any amazing accomplishments, let alone someone to share them with while flying at the speed of light in the farthest depths of space humans have ever traveled. But I hold out hope, you know? That years from now, before my life reaches its end, the mission can be successful, and I'll have something to show for myself when new people get here and take over this ship. At the moment it feels like there is very little here to indicate that the ship didn't just fly itself here without any crew at all."

Rick became silent.

"I don't want to keep telling you this. You have to stop your negativity. If I allow myself to think that my presence here holds no value, then I, and the mission, will fail. We both know this ship wasn't designed to be bullet proof. They didn't have the time to program and test every single aspect of the ship, or teleporter, or any of that stuff. They have no real idea what the new planet will actually be like. We were supposed to be the brains for the ship. We're the insurance that when things randomly break or something goes wrong that the mission is still viable. Plus, we both know how impossible things were getting on Earth. If they had tried adding a million more features to automate the ship, then they would have run out of time and money before the thing ever launched. The whole program was under constant scrutiny from the public, and the fruits of that very, very expensive labor were not obvious to the taxpayers paying for it."

Rick turned to Jason.

"I accept your apology. Now stop making things worse

and help me think. You know, when most people get bored or their daily lives feel too repetitive, they go on a trip. They visit a new place and try out new things. They inject excitement into their lives. I am simultaneously traveling more than anyone ever has in all of history and going no where at all. Ignoring all the other factors stacked against me, I feel like I could go insane from just the boredom. All work and no play makes Rick a dull boy."

Rick smiled at Jason, his smile returned by Jason's smolder.

"Chill out, dude. I'm not going to go on a rampage and start stabbing everyone... I don't think."

18 December 2510

Chapter 28

Rick arched his back sharply and winced. As the years went by it became more difficult to move after waking from the sleep chamber. His soreness reminded him of how he was changing even when his life felt like it was eternally stagnant. He looked at the display in his sleep chamber. He was 174 years into his journey, which meant he was now 197 years old.

He walked to the bathroom and began brushing his teeth. He allowed himself to look in the mirror, something he rarely did. Lines were beginning to grow on his face as he aged. His hair was now peppered with gray. His blue eyes had become dull over the years and were filled with resignation. Thanks to the sleep chamber, he didn't look any older than fifty-five. Though, he would begin to age faster as he used the chamber less, which he had to do now that he was getting older and his body was not able to rebound as quickly. He raked his fingers through his hair, stepped back from the mirror, and let out a disappointed grunt. *The only things that change are the things I wish would stay the same*, he thought.

He gradually made his way from the bathroom to his desk. He took the time to write down the dreams he had in as much detail as he could still remember. As he finished he gave a mournful sigh. It was time to get back to his normal routine. He got dressed and took a longing gaze at Jessica's portrait.

"I wish you were here."

. . .

"Alright guys, you know the routine. We've been asleep for a long time so we need to make the rounds and get the ship checked up," said Rick.

The portraits of the crew were lined up outside the front door of his house, waiting to report for duty.

"Jason, let's start by going and reviewing the ship's logs so we know that everything went well while we slept," said Rick as he picked up Jason's portrait and made his way to the cockpit.

"So how was your sleep Jason?" Rick floated into the cockpit and set Jason down near a control panel. "This can be just between the two of us, if you didn't sleep well. I just want to know the status of my crew."

He pressed buttons on the panel in front of him. "Okay, okay. I believe you, you're fine. How do you think Taisha is doing? I'm not sure if she would tell me if anything was wrong with her. She's the psychiatrist, after all. I bet she thinks she's impervious to trouble, or at least that any failings on her part would disqualify her from duty."

As lights flashed on the screen in front of him, everything read normal. "Everything looks good here, how about for you?" He went to where he had set Jason down and pressed buttons on the control panel. Lights quickly came to life.

"Everything is green, but does that look a little blurry to you?"

He squinted mildly and then turned to Jason.

"That's what I was afraid of. I may need to get glasses to diminish the degradation of my eye sight."

Rick paused.

"Yes, I know, glasses are archaic, but I just can't touch my own eyeball to put contacts on."

Rick finished his check up in the cockpit, picked up Jason, and began making his way back to the crew. "I shouldn't be surprised, I am getting older. Health issues are going to come up eventually. Minor health issues have been known to develop at an accelerated rate when using the sleep chamber too often, and that comes from limited studies since the tech is so new. Reality could actually be far worse than what the studies were able to reveal."

Rick paused and looked at the photo of Jason.

"I don't know if carrots actually improve your eyesight, but, you're right. I might as well try eating more of them."

...

"Without someone to properly examine my eyes, there is no way for me to know if I have developed astigmatism or not. However, I was reading the directions for the phoropter and it mentioned that having proper glasses can alleviate or even reverse astigmatism, so hopefully that will be enough," said Rick as he made himself lunch.

Matt's picture sat on the counter near Rick.

"Luckily, my blood work shows that everything else is still running strong. It definitely makes me wonder. Even though getting the right glasses is no big deal, what am I going to do if something goes wrong with me that I can't treat on my own?"

Rick picked Matt up and carried him to a table where he sat down to eat, Matt's energetic smile working to pacify Rick's concerns.

"Something as simple as throwing my back out could get me killed."

Rick ate his sandwich quickly. "It's amazing that despite the growth of technology, they couldn't, or didn't have time to, automate this whole process. I have to live for this mission to succeed. Without me, the teleporter won't turn on." He paused and listened to Matt.

"The problem is that it takes energy from one of the engines to power the thing and as a safety precaution it can't take that power automatically, just in case we are using all of the power for something important at the moment it wants to turn on. As far as why we needed to be here, it was an issue of time constraints, an inability to test, and the desire to have someone available to trouble shoot."

...

Rick gave out a little yip as a gush of air blew into his eye. "Taisha, don't laugh. This is really hard to do when I know it's coming." On his fifth attempt the machine made a valid measurement. A computer nearby chimed, the message on screen indicated his lenses would be ready in an hour.

"I guess I have time to do a second review of the results from my blood labs while I wait." He moved to a nearby computer and pulled up his results. "Well, I can't say I'm surprised," he said after skimming his results. "It's nearly impossible to be unhealthy with the ingredients we have on the ship, and I rarely take the time to cook something tasty enough to be bad for me."

Rick turned to Taisha.

"Yeah, everything looks the same. I didn't miss any details. Now help me pick frames for my glasses."

He rolled his chair over to a drawer and let out a disapproving "hmm" as he examined the contents.

"Looks like there are two styles to pick from: thin and thick. Beyond that, there are different colors for each style. What do you think, green or black?"

He turned to Taisha and swapped out the two frames on his face, back and forth. He watched her smile intently.

"I agree. The green is a bit more fun." He placed the black ones back in the drawer. With the green ones on, he turned and faced the mirror.

"It's nice to see a change when I look in the mirror that I'm actually in control of." Rick pulled the skin on his face with his finger tips to smooth out lines that had deepened over the years. He then brushed his hair back and examined his hairline, which was still strong but nonetheless diminished. After a moment he conceded with a dismissive shrug.

"Time goes on whether I like it or not, so I might as well enjoy the ride as much as I can." He gave one more glance at the mirror while combing his hair. "I could use a hair cut though."

22 September 2512
Chapter 29

Rick sat in the simulation room and watched the stars from outside change on the screens around him. He would often attempt to connect the stars into shapes while he waited for the images to update. He picked the brightest star he could find and drew in the air with his finger to create a shape. The star he used this time was directly behind the ship.

The screen refreshed. The brightest star was still the one he had just used, though the stars around it had changed significantly. He drew a horse as quickly as he could, and then the screen changed again. The bright star appeared in the same location behind the ship. Rick watched it as he waited for the screen to refresh again. When the new images appeared he noticed that despite the star being behind the ship, it was actually getting larger.

"That's impossible," said Rick to himself. He quickly got up, ran to the teleporter, and went to the cockpit. He pulled up the images he had just been seeing on the screens in front of him.

Over the next several screen refreshes he watched as the light grew larger until it eventually reached the edge of his ship. It appeared to be roughly twice the size of the space shuttle he had in the docking bay. It was a perfect sphere, and the light that it emanated was bright enough that no details could be seen on its surface. As it came closer to the docking bay, the controls and displays in front of Rick began to flicker and behave wildly.

"Incoming radio transmission," announced the computer over the intercom.

Radio transmission should be impossible at light speed, thought Rick, *though perhaps, since they are inside the light wave that the ship creates, their radio transmissions could go through.* Rick's mind raced madly. The screens in front of him continued to flicker.

"Incoming radio transmission," announced the intercom again.

He finally answered the transmission.

His radio was filled with static and squeals, reminding him of being in school when a history teacher played the sound of an internet connection over a phone line. Immediately, a siren rang and red lights began flashing. The display in front of Rick flashed a warning: "Docking bay doors are opening."

Rick turned around to see the safety door to the docking bay slam shut in anticipation of the air breach. He slammed on the controls, but was unable to override what was happening. His ship was about to be boarded.

A second announcement was made over the intercom. "System virus detected. Diagnosing."

He waited impatiently as the sirens rang around him. Watching the monitors, he could see the sphere approaching until it went out of view. He was unable to change camera angles to see what was happening because they were all pointed away from the docking bay doors. In frustration he moved away from the control panel and went to the sealed door. Gently he pressed his ear to it in hopes of being able to hear what was happening on the other side. He could hear nothing.

Suddenly, as he waited the main lights went out and the hallway was dimly lit with emergency lighting. The sirens stopped, indicating that the docking bay doors were closed. The hallway door leading to the docking bay opened, flooding the hallway with light.

"System virus removed. System restore in progress, estimated time of completion is one hour."

Rick moved into the docking bay carefully. The room was brightly lit from the visiting spacecraft. The massive spherical ship floated inside the docking bay, nearly touching the floor and ceiling. A door extended from its surface to create a ramp for exiting the ship. Rick saw no one in the room. He examined the ship cautiously as he approached it. He moved around the ship slowly so he could peer into it.

The ship appeared empty. He glanced around quickly to see if someone was hiding that he hadn't noticed before, but he still saw no one. He spoke to himself quietly, encouraging himself to go inside the ship for a closer examination.

The design of everything in the spacecraft seemed clearly alien to Rick, yet he was still able to recognize many of the elements he was looking at. The ship was quite odd to him. He was unable to determine the purpose of it. It was too small to be a vessel used for long distances, yet it had four sleep chambers in it. He opened several cabinets. All were filled with what Rick assumed was food. Finally he reached a large metallic cabinet that contained many guns.

If this were an emergency escape vessel, then why was it filled with so many guns, Rick thought to himself. Even if they were for self-defense and they somehow anticipated being overtaken by an enemy ship, as he just learned was possible, why would they take the offensive move of boarding a potentially hostile ship themselves.

He knew he didn't have time to waste analyzing the purpose of the spacecraft. There were potentially four aliens with guns on his ship.

"I'm just having a hallucination," he said to himself reassuringly. "But how can I know that for sure? I'm standing inside an alien spaceship. Seems pretty real to me, and if none of this is real then there is no loss. But if there are aliens on this ship and I pretend like nothing is happening, then I could be killed."

Rick swore to himself as he realized that by entering the alien spacecraft he had taken his eyes off of the door to the rest of the ship. They could be anywhere on the ship now. He grabbed a gun off of the weapon rack. The display came to life as he picked it up. He examined the screen, but was unable to tell what the various shapes indicated. He braced the weapon in his hands. As he rested his finger on the trigger, a small beam of light extended out from the end of the gun. "So that's how I aim," he whispered to himself.

He slowly exited the ship and looked around to see if he was alone. He had no idea what his intruders looked like, though the sleep chambers appeared to accommodate someone up to two and a half meters tall. The docking bay looked to be empty.

He inched forward, carefully allowing the gun he held to lead the way. He made sure not to set his finger on the trigger so that the laser sight would not give away his position. He first moved to the teleporter and disabled all teleporters from use without an authorization code. He then exited the docking bay and sealed the door behind him. The last thing he wanted to worry about was the intruders making their way into an area he had already cleared.

It took only a moment to clear and seal the cockpit, which he was relieved was empty, because it was the room hostiles could do the most damage from. From the control panel in the cockpit he then sealed all the doors to each section of the ship. Much of the ship's functionality had not been brought back online yet from the system reboot, but surveillance was running. Reviewing the video, he could see four large entities enter the Agrosim, they had not left before he had locked all the doors.

He was unsure how to get them out of the Agrosim and he was terrified that they may destroy his crops. He knew there was no way that he would be able to kill them with force since he was outnumbered and they were likely more tactical than he could be since he had no combat training. He decided his only hope was to lure them back to their ship and eject them out the way they came.

Returning to the docking bay, he found whatever tools he could and began dismantling the electronics of the visiting shuttle so that it would not be able to hijack the electronics of his ship again and hopefully would also not be able to start. He did not stop destroying their ship until he was sure they would be stranded. Once he was done he made his way to the crew quarters and barricaded the doors. It would not stop them from getting in, but it would hopefully discourage them enough to look for somewhere else to go.

Finally, he made his way back to the cockpit and sealed the door behind him. He watched the video monitors of the Agrosim, but he could not see them. He then opened the door from the Agrosim to the crew quarters. He waited for the aliens to emerge, but, no matter how long he waited, they did not move. After twenty minutes he realized he would have to do something to lure them out.

Rick exited the cockpit and secured the door behind him. The door would only open with his voice command. He made his way to the Agrosim. He could see as he approached that some branches had been broken and were lying on the ground, and he knew that was likely from them climbing into the trees for hiding.

He drew his weapon forward as he neared the door. He couldn't see any movement inside the room. He waited outside of the Agrosim hoping that his presence alone would draw them out so that he would not have to enter.

"Come out here! Stop hiding!" He yelled, in an attempt to provoke them. He waited for a response. Nothing happened. Impatiently he decided he would have to enter the room.

He approached the door cautiously, his heart pounding in his chest. The room felt dimly lit under the shade of many tall trees. He entered slowly, scanning the area for movement repeatedly as he inched forward. After making it several steps into the room, he paused and listened carefully. He still saw and heard nothing. He continued further into the room.

He quickly reached some fallen branches. He glanced down at the branches so he would not trip, and noticed a small red dot crawling across a branch. He immediately turned around to run away when a flash of light shot out from above him from within the trees and struck the ground where he had been moving toward. A small explosion shook Rick and threw him to the ground. He looked back to see the branches largely missing or burnt, but the ground beneath it fully intact.

"The guns only hurt organic life," he said to himself.

Rick jumped to his feet as he saw the red light on the ground begin to move closer to him again. He escaped the Agrosim as quickly as he could for a moment of safety, and in hopes that he would prevent them from doing more damage to the plants on the ship. He ran to the airlock in the hallway leading to the cockpit and waited for the aliens to emerge. He heard noise from within the Agrosim as he pointed his gun at the door.

After a short moment of waiting, a large creature appeared at the door. It was almost two and a half meters tall, with the upper body of a gorilla, and the parts of the upper body that were not covered in armor were covered in hair. The lower body was shaped like the back-end of a horse, though the hooves appeared much stockier than a horse. Without hesitation, Rick shot at the creature. The blast from the gun threw him backward into the tunnel. The creature let out a yell, but Rick didn't wait to see the alien's condition. He returned to the cockpit and watched the monitors to see what the aliens did next.

Three more aliens emerged from the plants and examined their fallen companion. They quickly became enraged and ran in the direction of the cockpit. Without lingering, they followed the path that Rick had made for them. They entered the docking bay and began searching the area. Rick seized the opportunity and sealed the door, locking them in the docking bay. He then triggered the docking bay doors to open.

A warning siren rang over the intercom and Rick

watched the monitors as the aliens scrambled to their ship for safety. The doors slowly opened and Rick watched in shock as the alien ship didn't move. He then remembered that the ship, while at full speed, creates a bubble that prevents a quick vacuum from sucking everything out of the ship. Fear began creeping in as he worried about how he may have to close the bay doors and enter the docking bay to create a way to propel the alien spacecraft out of his ship.

As fear of the situation began to overwhelm him, he realized the solution was much easier than he could have hoped for. He triggered a test of the core engines which temporarily slows the ship, not enough to feel it if you are in an area of the ship with simulated gravity but enough to move you if you are floating in zero-gravity. As the test activated, he could see over the monitor as the alien spacecraft began to move forward as the ship slowed. It crawled forward until it bumped into a workbench and began drifting backward. As the test ended the ship resumed its previous speed and the alien spacecraft moved toward the open bay doors more quickly.

As the spacecraft left the docking bay Rick joyfully closed the bay doors. He took a moment to laugh at the absurdity of the situation, knowing that none of it could possibly have happened. He decided to write everything down in his journal and then go to bed, ignoring the dead alien that lay just inside the Agrosim.

28 February 2514
Chapter 30

Rick looked down at a sea of leaves, still and unchanging like a photograph. His stomach struggled to remember that he was not at risk of falling as he floated thirty meters in the air with gravity off, despite the view. He maneuvered a large light bulb into place and began reattaching the glass cover. He had procrastinated on replacing the lights in the Agrosim until the third one burned out. The produce was beginning to suffer from the lack of simulated sunlight.

He took in his surroundings and made sure all the lights were now working correctly again. He then gathered his tools and floated back to the ground. At the control panel, near the entrance to the Agrosim, he navigated the menus on screen until it prompted him with, "Resume gravitational rotation?" and confirmation buttons. He selected yes.

A buzzer rang over the intercom. "Two minutes until resumed gravitational rotation. Please secure all large objects."

After two minutes, the intercom beeped again as gravity was reactivated. Rick's feet slowly touched the ground. As pressure began resting on him again, it reminded him of an elevator slowly beginning its ascent. He walked back into the Agrosim and stood underneath one of the lights he had replaced. From this distance he couldn't actually inspect his handiwork. Yet somehow, standing in the light that the new bulb was creating, seemed sufficient.

He looked around at the extra light that now illuminated his surroundings. As he stood there he heard a small *crack* and a moment later heard rustling in the trees next to him. Over the years he had learned to not overreact to his hallucinations as they started, so he calmly looked around. He tried to think of how he could determine if he were hallucinating right now.

Suddenly there was a much louder cracking sound that seemed to come from above him. He looked up and struggled to make out what he was looking at in the bright light. Before he had a chance to react, the glass panel that was supposed to cover the light he had last changed struck his arm just below his right shoulder, threw him to the ground, and landed on his arm.

Rick screamed in agony. The pain was so strong that he was terrified to look at the injury, though he knew he had no choice. His arm was pinned under the glass panel. He blindly tried shoving on the panel with his free arm, but it was far too heavy and pulled on his pinned arm, creating pain so sharp that he risked passing out. He knew he would have to gather the courage to look at his arm.

His arm was ripped more than halfway through just past the elbow. A sliver of muscle and some skin were all that appeared to be holding his arm together. Blood gushed from his arm and he knew he didn't have much time. Looking around him, he found his bush trimmers nearby. Adrenaline slowly set in as he opened the trimmers and carefully maneuvered them. He paused for a moment, took several deep breaths, and then screamed as loud as he could as he slammed the trimmers closed. The contents of his arm gave little resistance to the blades, and with that, he was free. He then removed his belt and wrapped it around his arm to limit the bleeding.

As he scrambled to his feet. The loss of blood made him feel light-headed, his vision going in and out of focus. Judging from the amount of blood he saw around him, he had only moments to get to Medical and stop the bleeding. His mind and thoughts became distant and detached from the body that was struggling for survival, observing himself in seemingly third-person. He began to accept the likelihood of his own demise.

01 March 2514

Chapter 31

Rick enjoyed the feeling of the warm water rushing between his toes as he stood, staring out at the expanse before him. The sound of the foamy waves rushing onto the shore before pulling away as quickly as they came was rhythmic and soothing. The water stretched out endlessly. As he became more aware of where he was, he looked around to see if anyone else was on the beach or if he was alone.

On either side of him the beach appeared to be empty, and the dense forest behind him was foreboding and impossible to see far enough into to know what might be hiding in there. He dared not stare too long at the forest behind him in fear that it might provoke something that wouldn't have otherwise happened. He directed his attention back to the ocean before him.

Feeling a moment of peace, he sat down in the sand and allowed the water to gently wash over his feet, continually threatening to climb higher before retreating around the same distance. He closed his eyes and listened to the waves and the wind that rushed through his hair and clothes in random short bursts. The sun had an intensity that warmed his skin and revitalized him in a way that he hadn't felt in years.

As he rested on the sand enjoying the experience, he heard a splash in the water nearby. He opened his eyes to examine his surroundings. He still saw no one and could not see any fish or water creature that would have made the sound. As he looked in the water to his left he heard a splash to his right.

He stood and turned to examine the area, yet still saw nothing. He squinted to focus his vision and attempted to see through the water. Suddenly something struck him from behind. He clutched at his back as he turned around and looked at the ground to find a small rock. As he bent over to pick it up, he heard the sound of another rock flying by his head and hitting the water behind him. He brought the hand that had been rubbing his back forward, and saw that the stone had drawn blood. The blood felt cold as it dripped down his back and the wind blew through his shirt.

The stones began appearing more frequently, and though he couldn't tell where exactly they were coming from, he could tell that they were coming from multiple directions. He ran down the beach in an attempt to escape the stones that were being thrown at him. No matter how far he ran, the stones kept coming and they were becoming more accurate and painful. His attackers, however, remained hidden in the forest.

After running for several minutes and not escaping the stones or finding a place to hide, he turned and ran into the water. He swam as fast as he could, continually hearing the stones splash behind him. He swam until he no longer heard any noise other than from himself. He turned around to watch the beach and see if the stone throwers would reveal themselves, and was shocked by how far he had to swim to escape them. *They must have been using slingshots or a gun*, he thought. He was easily 100 meters away from the shore.

He waded in the water for a while, watching the shore. He was beginning to feel fatigued from all of his exertion and knew he would need to return to shore soon. As he swam in the water, debating with himself about when it would be safe to swim back, he felt something brush against his leg. He could see where the land took a steep dive beneath the water. He was too far out for it to be any plant that would have brushed against him. Then he remembered the injury on his back, and the other spots he had been hit by stones that were likely bleeding as well. A new fear swelled up within him, pulling from deep wells rooted in his childhood. Sharks.

He looked in all directions, attempting to see if any shark fins had broken the surface, but he didn't see any. As he searched, the shark slammed into his leg with more force this time. He began swimming back to shore. He knew stones were less dangerous. He swam as quickly as he could until something yanked him back. He screamed in pain and inhaled water as the shark sank its teeth into his leg. He wanted to fight the shark, but found himself too busy drowning from the water he had inhaled.

Suddenly released, he struggled to reach the surface. Instinctively, he coughed repeatedly in an attempt to reject the water from his lungs. His body's natural effort proved fruitless. He could not use his bitten leg enough to breach the water for a breath of air, but instead inhaled even more water. His lungs burned as they struggled to survive without oxygen. Finally, from exhaustion and pain, he gave up and allowed himself to sink.

The water around him quickly grew into a dark, consuming blue. He watched as the sun above the water faded away, and he was surrounded by the black of the deep abyss.

05 March 2514

Chapter 32

Rick awoke to the machine next to him beeping loudly in his ear. The shrill noise pulling him painfully from a deep slumber. Cords from the machine that stood beside him ran down along his bed and into his arm. He lay on pure white sheets that were thoroughly covered in his blood, though he had no energy or desire to change them. The hospital room he was recovering in was painted a light sea foam color and appeared calming and inviting.

He carefully got out of his hospital bed and replaced the empty bag connected to his IV. He vaguely remembered getting to the hospital and treating his arm, but had no idea how he got his IV in. The artificial skin he had used to cover the wound, combined with the bandages, had eliminated any major continuing risks from his injuries, though he still had to be extremely careful of infections. After fixing his IV and replacing his bandages, he gently laid back down in bed.

He let out a deep sigh and turned to look at the picture of Linda that lay on the night stand next to him, her playfully fanned hair, vibrant eyes, and thoughtful smile comforting him. Much like his IV, he had no idea how she had gotten there. "You know, this incident really puts the mission at risk."

He paused and stared at Linda.

"I appreciate the encouraging words, but it's true. I'm going to die at a younger age now. The life expectancy of a left handed person is four to five years less than a right handed person."

Rick paused.

"I'm being completely serious. I'm pretty sure I even read it on the internet once," he said, unable to prevent himself from cracking a smile. "I'm sure having an amputation doesn't help either."

Rick pressed a button that rested beside him, increasing his pain medication. He laid his head back and closed his eyes. "I'm glad you're here Linda, we haven't spent much time together before, this is nice."

...

After two weeks of keeping himself hooked up to hospital monitors, he decided he was well enough to leave. He removed his IV, made his bed, and picked up Linda. His right arm was heavily bandaged and he knew it was a wound that would take a long time to fully heal. The small nub that extended past his elbow seemed as though it would still move, but it also felt to him that even looking at it made it hurt. He was hoping that it would eventually be something he could still use.

"I think I'm finally stable enough that I can leave this place without worrying, and boy am I glad. Though, I'm not that happy that I'm leaving one prison cell for another, but I know I can do the best healing with the least amount of pain if I jump into the sleep chamber. When I wake up again, my arm will be healed and I can start doing my rehab. Also, I'm a bit bummed. I've always heard stuff about people being able to still feel their limb after they lose it. That didn't happen to me. I was hoping it might give me some connection to the afterlife. Oooooo," he said in a ghostly voice.

Rick looked at Linda's picture.

"Alright, I'll take things seriously. You don't need to roll your eyes at me. It does mean a lot to me, though, that you were with me this whole time. I'm glad to know at least one person on this ship cares about me." Rick suddenly remembered the thousands of years that had passed on Earth and Shadow Space Colony since he had last been there. "I guess not just on this ship. The only people who know who I am, or possibly even know I exist at all are on this ship."

Rick shook his head to clear his thoughts. He walked over to a nearby intercom, realized he needed to set Linda down to free his hand, and activated the intercom. "I want all personnel lined up outside of my house in five minutes," he said, and then turned off the intercom. He faced Linda, "I'm getting used to being left-handed, but I'm nowhere near remembering I only have one hand yet. I'll escort you to the lineup."

He picked up her picture again and used the teleporter in his hospital room to go to his house. Outside his house the pictures were lined up, though some had fallen over from the zero gravity of Rick changing the light bulbs in the Agrosim.

"You guys refused to come see me in the hospital, and I come here to find you all just lying around. I'm truly hurt." Rick walked to the tipped-over pictures and placed them upright, giving each a stern look as he repositioned them. "I've learned through this that Linda is the only one I can depend on. And you know what? That's fine, I guess I will

05 March 2514

just spend my time with someone who is there for me."

Rick paced for a moment as he shook his head in disappointment. "I'm going into the sleep chamber to heal. I know it is risky since the muscles in my arm might heal in a tightened position, but it is the safest and least painful way to heal while avoiding using significant amounts of pain meds. I'll just have to adjust the muscle stimulation on my arm to help things heal properly and start rehab after I wake up. I know you obviously didn't find me, or my condition, very important, so I won't bore you with details, but please at least look after the ship while I am asleep."

Rick turned away and walked into his home. A sudden sense of déjà vu rushed over him as he remembered the first time he entered his home after his crew had died. The painful realization that his life had just been changed forever and that he was going to have to work hard to create a new normal threatened to overwhelm him. He made his way upstairs quickly, desiring to escape his physical and emotional turmoil in his sleep chamber. As he entered his room he saw his guitar leaning in the corner. He walked to it and gently set his hand on it. He gave it a light tap to acknowledge that this source of joy had now ended before lying down in his sleep chamber.

02 April 2514
Chapter 33

"Honey, wake up. We don't have much time."

Rick gently opened the lid to his sleep chamber. He was inside the apartment he and Jessica shared before they had left on the ship. He looked around and was surprised by how vividly he remembered their old bedroom.

Despite all of the dreams he'd had, this was the first one where he knew he was sleeping. He looked at Jessica, who was standing outside his sleep chamber waiting for him, and smiled. Her green eyes stared at him intently, pulling him toward her with excitement.

"Sweetie, you need to get up quickly. I have plans for us," she said to him urgently.

He couldn't remember the last time he had a dream where Jessica was in it and she wasn't hostile to him. He got out of his sleep chamber happily and dressed himself. He was willing to comply with anything she said. He didn't want to let her know he was dreaming and risk ending the experience.

"What do you have planned? Is it a movie? I know how much you love cuddling in front of a movie." Rick responded joyfully.

"No, we're getting out of here," she replied quickly.

"Like for a walk?" He couldn't think where they would go. "I didn't think you cared for walks that much."

"I just figured it was time for a change," said Jessica as

she yanked him to his feet after he finished getting his shoes on. She held his hand tightly and gave him a tug as she moved to the front door. Her fiery hair swayed hypnotically as she moved, stirring memories within Rick he hadn't realized he longed to experience again.

As they exited their apartment, Rick began rummaging through his pockets to find his keys to lock their door.

"Don't worry about it," said Jessica as she pulled him away and began down the brightly lit hallway outside their apartment. Her soft hand and firm, reassuring grip pulled not just his body but his heart with her.

"All of the restaurants are in the other direction. Are we not going to eat?"

"No, I just want the two of us to be alone, if we can find some place for that," she replied as she walked briskly.

"Then why aren't we just staying at the apartment? It was just you and me."

"I know they will be there soon. Look, don't worry about it, honey. We're just going for a walk and spending some nice time together. Can you just let me have that, please?" Her eyes pleaded with him as she spared him a glance while moving forward.

"Whatever will make you happy. I'm just glad we are together." Rick became afraid that he might upset her and change his dream into a nightmare, so he chose to not ask questions.

They reached the end of the hallway, which had several elevators. Jessica pulled them into one that was open and pressed the button for ground level. The elevator moved slowly, and Jessica was noticeably irritable with its pace. After two floors, she pressed a button for the next floor.

"I can't believe how slow this elevator is moving. It feels like it's crawling. We'll just get out and take the stairs."

As the doors opened Jessica peeked out and looked in both directions. She then pulled Rick in the direction of the stairs.

"We're still eight floors up, that's a lot of stairs. Is everything okay?" Rick asked as he entered the stairwell. His voice bounced loudly around him.

"Don't worry about it. The exercise could do you some good."

They were met with two doors when they reached the first floor. One led to the front entry of the building and the other was an exit to the side of the building.

"Perfect, we can finally get outside," said Jessica as she flung the door open.

The apartment building they lived in was part of student housing located on the HIEPE campus. The campus was a four square kilometer area surrounded by a large wall. The teachers explained that it was never intended to give off the perception of isolation or exclusion, but was built for the sake of safety from a fluctuating world perception of well-being. As the world economy suffered and the cost of living rose, they anticipated that the security that HIEPE provided its students would come under attack. However, the wall had many roads and doors that currently remained open at all times. Students and faculty could come and go as they pleased, though it was discouraged.

"Let's go for a walk in the park," said Jessica.

Directly behind their apartment building was a large park with walking paths that were surrounded by trees. Jessica pulled on his arm as she jogged to the nearest path. The trees that lined the path were large and close enough together that they hid the large wall that was less than 100 meters ahead of them.

Jessica looked around, Rick didn't know for what, and she slowed to a calm walk as she found that they were alone. She noticed Rick looking at her, confused. "They are about to get us and tell us it's time to leave for our trip and I just wanted a little more time with you before everything changes, that's all," she said with a smile. She drew him closer to her and embraced his arm as they walked together. Her warmth and soft bosom pressed against him sent waves of peace, comfort, and acceptance through him, revealing the painful deprivation he had been enduring.

"I wish this trip had never happened to us," said Jessica quietly. "Imagine what our lives could have been like had we just been able to go and do whatever we wanted."

"I think about that every day," said Rick sadly.

"I know you do. You've always been so romantic. What's your favorite thought?" asked Jessica.

"I usually imagine that we would have lived in a two story house near a lot of shopping, like a mall."

"I haven't been to a mall in ages!" exclaimed Jessica.

As they walked Rick could hear men talking loudly and approaching from behind. Jessica sped up their pace.

"Would we go there often?" She asked, masking her concern for the approaching men behind them.

"Every weekend. We would window shop or see a movie," replied Rick as Jessica reached a full run.

They cut off the path, through the trees, toward the perimeter wall of the complex. They ran toward a door that was directly ahead of them.

"Saturday date night sounds wonderful," said Jessica as she reached the door and threw it open.

The men behind them were getting closer as Rick looked over his shoulder. Before he knew what was happening, Jessica pulled him through the door and he was immediately met with the noise of a large crowd.

Rick looked around in amazement at the food court that surrounded him. Looking behind him, the door they had entered had transformed into a tinted glass door that led to a very full parking lot.

"I can see how this would be great," said Jessica in a mild yell. The food court was very loud with many people sitting around talking and music playing over the intercom. "Even in your dreams you do what I want," said Jessica with a smile. "I know you don't like this many people or this much noise."

"That's why we would usually end the evening with a movie," replied Rick.

They walked through the food court and reached the stores of the mall. The noise quickly died down as they distanced themselves from the food court.

"So what stores would we go in as we walk through the mall?"

"Whichever would make you the happiest," Rick replied as he put his arm around her.

"I'm not a tyrant that makes you do whatever I want, am I? We would at least look at some stores for music or video games, right?"

"Honey, of course you're not a tyrant. Sometimes you would humor me and let me go into a video game store, but that's not why we are here. Is there anything here that I wouldn't just buy online? Do I really care about walking around a mall for my own amusement? Sure, people watching is fun, but I can actually get a better view of you when we are at home" said Rick as he gave her a wink.

"If you are only looking at me then it's person watching, not people watching. But it's very sweet of you to make such sacrifices for my happiness."

They turned into a jewelry store and began looking at all of the diamond rings.

"I do wish we could have experienced so much more," said Jessica as she looked at the diamonds in front of her.

As they paused and looked, they heard some men at the other end of the store begin talking loudly. Jessica and Rick looked up and saw two men behind a counter pointing at them as they spoke angrily.

"They found us Rick! Quick, let's go."

They exited the store quickly and made their way through the large crowds of people in the mall.

"There are too many people here. As fun as it would be to do something totally different, I don't think I would like this for very long. What else do you like imagining our lives would be like?" Asked Jessica as they pushed their way through the people ahead of them.

"I thought about how we could travel the world. Why be stuck in just one place when we could go everywhere?"

They ran toward a nearby wall with a door that led to a stairwell. Rick could hear men yelling from behind him. He could not see their pursuers in the thick crowd of people as Jessica pulled him through the door.

As he turned around he saw rows of seats ahead of him. They were on an airplane.

Looking behind him he saw that they had come through the bathroom door. Some of the passengers looked at them sternly as they exited the back cabin of the plane. They quickly sat in the first open seats they found.

"Traveling the world would be amazing," said Jessica as she peered out the window at the clouds below. "Every day we could wake up in a different bed and see something new. We could actually see the history of our world, rather than just reading about it."

Rick struggled to adjust his armrest so that he could get closer to Jessica. As they embraced each other, Jessica attempted to recline her chair to be more comfortable.

"As great as it would be to see the world with you, I don't know if I could give up having a place to call home. I still feel like this would be a sacrifice you would make to make me happy."

Rick kissed her gently on her forehead. "There isn't a sacrifice I'm not willing to make to make you happy."

They both peeked over the backs of their chairs as they heard a commotion from the cabin behind them. They quickly began exiting the row they were sitting in.

"Where can we go Rick? Where can we go that they won't find us?" asked Jessica urgently. "Where else would you want to go? Somewhere that would make you happy."

Two men emerged from the cabin behind them. They forcefully pushed the people and carts in front of them out of their way.

"The place I always wanted to go with you the most was an island. No specific island, just somewhere where we are alone together," said Rick as they made their way forward on the plane.

"That sounds great," said Jessica with excitement as she turned sharply down a row of seats and began opening the escape hatch.

Rick watched the men behind them get ever closer as a gust of wind sucked him out of the door as Jessica opened it. He felt the sensation of falling for a moment and abruptly landed on his back. As he opened his eyes he saw the island he had seen in many dreams before. The plane was nowhere in sight. He turned to look for Jessica and found her nearby getting to her feet.

"Do you think we are safe here?" asked Jessica.

"I don't know, but I wouldn't go into the jungle," replied Rick.

"Have you been here before?"

He didn't answer. He turned to look out at the water and saw that the sun was beginning to set. "We better get some wood and start a fire before the sun goes down."

"Okay."

He was relieved that Jessica stayed close to him as he gathered wood.

"This definitely seems like the place that would be the best for us," said Jessica as she picked up some dry branches from the ground. "It's perfect for you because it's just us on the island, no noise, no obligations, no rush. And it's exactly what I want because every direction I look is beautiful."

"I know how much you always wished you had been to a tropical beach," said Rick as he started to pile the wood he had gathered for the fire.

Jessica looked at the sun that began to touch the horizon. "We don't have much time, do we?"

Rick found two stones to start the fire with. "Maybe

twenty minutes."

Jessica walked behind him as he approached the pile of wood and rested her head on his back as she gently embraced him. "I don't want you to wake up."

He paused, shocked to realize that Jessica knew she was in his dream. His eyes began to feel heavy as the exhaustion of their running caught up to him. "Let's just start this fire so we have light and warmth and just enjoy the moment we have left."

He bent over and scraped the rocks together until a spark lit the pile of sticks. By the time the fire had grown, the sun had completely set. The moon hung large and bright in the distance, allowing them to see the water rushing back and forth across the sand. They cuddled close to each other and enjoyed the warmth of the fire.

"I'm getting really tired, Rick," said Jessica, sadly.

"I know. I am too."

"Are you going to be here when I wake up?" She asked as she turned to face him.

"No."

"Do you think this is the last time we'll be together?"

"I don't know. I've waited more years than I can imagine for this moment. I have no reason to believe that I will ever be this fortunate again."

Jessica kissed him softly on the lips and then rested her head on his chest. He traced his finger along the shape of her face, admired the light freckles of her nose and cheeks, caressed her soft lips and the delicate point of her chin. Lingering as long as possible on the beauty that he craved more of. He embraced her and laid his head down on the sand. He looked at the stars for as long as he was able to keep his eyes open, soaking in the sound of the waves and the gentle movement of Jessica's breathing. When the weight of his fatigue became more than he could bear, he closed his eyes.

07 June 2514

Chapter 34

Rick held the picture of Jessica in his hand. His face was expressionless as he processed the dream he just had. Her arresting green eyes, warm smile, and voluminous hair sparked a yearning in his heart that ached it.

"I know I'm nearly gone. Every time I leave this room, that voice inside my head that reminds me I am alone and my conversations are with myself gets smaller and smaller. Any day could be my last and I'm glad that I got to share my last fully aware moment with you. And yet…"

Rick set her picture down on the dresser in front of him. His face, fraught with sadness. "The little bit of reality you bring back into my life hurts more than the fear of losing myself forever. The truth is, when I'm out there, I don't know that anything is wrong with me. When I come back here, that's when fear tries to take over." Rick paused and thought about his next words. "As much as I want you with me, I need to leave you here."

As he walked down the stairs toward his front door, his burden of awareness slowly drifted away. With each step came a stronger sense of peace until he finally opened his front door and saw his crew lined up, waiting for him. He smiled.

"I'm glad to see you guys are awake and ready. I hope the time you all had in your sleep chambers was pleasant."

Rick paused.

"My arm seems to have healed quite well while I was sleeping. Thanks for asking Linda. Speaking of which, I want to get everything done quickly for check-ups because I will need to start rehab. Linda, I'm assuming you will want to come since you have been so supportive thus far. Anything anyone needs to say before we get started?"

Rick looked back and forth between the pictures.

"No? Good. And listen, I've decided to forgive you all for not visiting me. I understand that everyone was probably really busy maintaining the ship while I was in the hospital, especially with Linda also looking after me. Let's just put it behind us, alright? Time for us to get to work!"

Rick picked up Jason's photo and made his way to the cockpit.

. . .

"What did you dream about while you were sleeping?" Rick asked as he stretched on a yoga mat for his rehab.

Linda's photo sat a few steps away from the mat Rick was on.

"Wow. Having all of your teeth fall out sounds terrifying. What were you doing when it happened?"

Rick glanced at Linda.

"Driving? Did you crash?"

Another pause.

"You swerved into oncoming traffic and woke up right before you crashed into another car? Maybe you were just stressed about how our success is largely dependent on the chemicals you produced to condition the soil on the new planet. Or it could be difficulty with a relationship that is bothering you."

"I understand how you could be stressed about the future. My arm obviously makes things a bit harder for me."

Rick finished his final stretches and then sprawled out on the exercise mat as he lay down. He turned his head to look at Linda.

"I think I'll be okay. I've been able to maintain most of the mobility of my upper arm and should be fine after a couple more weeks of rehab. I'll need to do more work on smaller activities since I've lost my dominant hand, but that will take time. Even little things like adjusting my glasses with my left hand feels a little weird, but obviously it isn't hard to do."

Rick grabbed Linda as he got up. "Thanks for coming with me, it was nice having you to talk with, but I have to go now. I promised Matt I would help him with the trimming in the Agrosim which is definitely going to take me longer to do than before since now I can only use the hand saw."

Rick left the doctor's office and made his way to the teleporter. Landing outside the homes, he returned Linda to the lineup of photos and picked up Matt.

"I'm going to need you to pull your own weight this time because I'm not sure how much trimming I can do with just one hand."

Rick walked to the transitioning room and waited for access to the Agrosim. He had stopped using the outfits that kept the moisture off of him a long time ago and thought about how hard that suit would be to put on with just one hand. He entered cautiously, forever afraid that another light housing might come crashing down on him.

The branches had grown significantly, since he had not

trimmed them since his accident. The only time he had entered the room since then was to clean up the remains of his arm. Blood could still be found in some spots that he had not thoroughly cleaned.

He laid the old tools he had previously used, that required two hands, next to Matt for him to use, and then retrieved the branch saw. He fumbled through cutting several branches, awkwardly attempting to balance the hilt of the pole under his right arm while keeping his left arm farther up the pole for the back and forth motion of cutting. By the time he figured out the best position to hold the branch saw, he was already exhausted. Both of his arms burned under the effort. He eventually had to give in to his fatigue and take a break. He sat down next to Matt.

"This might kill me if you don't help out more. The awkward twist I have to put myself through just to hold things properly is going to throw out my back," said Rick between gulps of breath. He turned to look at Matt.

"I don't know what Jessica is up to. I think she just refused to come out and help the rest of the crew. I'm not sure what's going on with her."

Rick scuffed his feet on the ground as he thought to himself.

"No, I don't think we've had any fights lately. I guess we are just growing apart. I mean, we all seem to be doing that a little bit. None of you guys came to visit me in the hospital, but it is worse that Jessica didn't show up either. Maybe we are all just getting tired of seeing the same faces day in and day out for years with no hope of change, and she just doesn't want to be around me or anyone else anymore."

Rick rested for a few more minutes in silence, drank some

water, and then resumed his work. He would have to put a lot of effort into this if he didn't want it getting away from him over time.

"How have you and Adelina been?" asked Rick in an attempt to distract himself from the exertion of his work.

"Steady as a rock, huh? That must be nice." Rick paused to wipe the sweat that drenched his face away from his eyes. "I'm happy for you guys. Just don't let her grow distant toward you. It can be hard to deal with."

Rick turned and looked at Matt.

"Oh dude, don't tell me things like that or I'm not going to be able to look at Adelina the same. I'm glad your love life is so healthy, but keep that to yourself. I interact with her way too much to know those kinds of things."

Rick shook his head.

"No, you're not being helpful. I don't think I'm even flexible enough to do that. You're just bragging," he said with a laugh.

16 January 2515
Chapter 35

Rick sat impatiently in the simulation room as he waited for Linda. He didn't care much for the beach simulation since he'd died on the beach many times in his dreams over the years, but Linda had said it was her favorite. He wiggled the watch on his wrist as he checked it. It was one of several ticks he had developed while learning to be left handed. He wasn't sure if he would ever get used to wearing his watch on his left wrist.

Finally, after waiting thirty minutes and finishing his lemonade, he realized she had stood him up. He angrily gathered his things and stormed out of the room to look for her. He eventually found her in the cockpit.

"What are you doing here? We had a date," he said, struggling to hide his frustration.

He waited for her answer. Her blue eyes looked at him wildly, suffocating him.

"What do you mean he knows? What did you tell him?" Rick picked up Linda and floated out of the cockpit and into medical for additional privacy.

"Don't you think he's overreacting? We've just been spending a lot of time together. Nothing's happened," he delivered in a harsh whisper.

He looked at her desperately. Her unchanging expression gave him no hope. "What do you mean we can't see each other anymore? He can't make that call. It's up to us to decide. I need this!"

Rick's face contorted in fear and panic. His anger pulsed through his muscles until he felt his bones would snap from the anxiety. Unable to think of anything else to do, he stormed off quickly to find Tim.

He entered the engineering room and found Tim waiting for him. He did his best to calm down before talking.

"Tim, listen. I don't know exactly what she told you, but I think you're overreacting. Nothing has happened between us. We've just been spending time together, that's all." He walked closer to Tim. "After everything that has happened to me, I'm still in a lot of pain. She's helped me stay distracted. She's made my recovery easier. You can't just take that away from me."

Rick stared at Tim as he paced back and forth.

"I will not let you boss me around, Tim. I am the captain of this ship, and I make the rules. You are subservient to me! Do not raise your voice with me!" Rick's voice spiked to a hoarse scream.

"Don't you dare try to take her from me!" He yelled through shaking anger.

In a rage he picked up Tim's picture and threw it, sending it across the room and shattering it on the ground. A sudden awareness of what he had just done struck him with sobriety. He panicked and ran to the picture. The shattered glass had scratched the photo in multiple places, deep lines that ran across Tim's face.

"You made me do this, Tim. Why did you make me do this? Now look at you. Everyone will know something happened between us. I can't let them see you like this. You'll tell them everything. Then everyone will abandon me."

Rick closed his eyes tightly and gripped the edge of the picture in his fingers.

"I didn't want this, but you made me." His voice shaky as a sudden urge to sob overtook him. He inhaled deeply. As he quickly exhaled he ripped the picture in half. "They can't ever know." He tore the picture again and again.

Rick's eyes welled with tears as the weight of what he had done set in. In desperate fear he searched the room for any witnesses. Not seeing anyone, he quickly grabbed the pieces of the picture and threw them into a nearby garbage shoot. He heard a *whoosh* as the picture was being sucked away.

Rick fell to his knees and wept. For the first time in many years, he felt alone. An emptiness and sense of isolation swept over him, sending a tingle down his back as the fear of loneliness threatened to cripple him. He jumped to his feet and began running to his sleep chamber. As he ran he could not shake the sudden feeling that he was being watched. He paused and stood at the exit of the Agrosim. He could see his home from where he stood. Despite his desire to escape from what he had just done, the presence he felt was so strong behind him that it burned the back of his mind to not look. As he turned around, he saw a shadowy figure. Rick rubbed his eyes, hoping that his failing eyesight could be proven to be the culprit of what he was seeing. The specter stood, waiting at the other end of the Agrosim. It was similar in shape and size to Rick and was almost entirely transparent, but what filled Rick with fear was the maddening feeling in his mind that the presence was there and watching him. He knew it must be Tim's ghost trying to get revenge. He stood watching for a couple of minutes, unsure of what would happen next. *He's just waiting for his moment.*

Without hesitation he turned back around and continued running to his sleep chamber. He never looked behind himself to see if the shadow was still following, but the anxious feeling he was suffering told him all he needed to know.

17 January 2515
Chapter 36

Rick felt the crack of a small stick on his back as he shuffled forward. His feet were chained together with just enough slack for small steps, while the soil, small brush, and broken branches he stepped on, dug into his bare feet. His hands were bound together in front of him with rope. He recognized the jungle he was currently marching in. Taking a look behind him, he could see the beach from so many of his previous dreams. He didn't remember the mountain he was currently climbing. He had never been to this part of the island.

Surrounding him were men in loin cloths that prodded him forward. Each man wore a loincloth and a mask of a face exaggeratedly depicting a different emotion. He was surprised by how white their skin was, and confused that if he imagined tribal men on an island to at least have a dark tan, then why wasn't that what his imagination had created?

"Where are you taking me?" Rick asked the man behind him, his mask depicting anger.

The man quickly slashed him with the branch he was holding, and, in a voice that sounded oddly familiar to Rick, said, "It is unwise for you to ask questions."

Rick frowned in disapproval at the man's reaction and faced forward. He gradually climbed the mountain he was on in silence. He wondered if this part of the island had always existed and he hadn't noticed, or if it was new to this dream. Suddenly a low rumbling noise emanated from ahead as the ground shook hard enough to knock him to his knees and a large cloud of smoke bellowed out of the mountain top.

"Are we climbing an active volcano?" asked Rick in alarm. Two men, one from each of Rick's sides came to him and lifted him to his feet. The man behind Rick prodded him to continue walking.

"The volcano has not erupted since our people came to this island hundreds of years ago," said another man behind Rick. The man's mask conveyed the emotion of jealousy. "But recently the volcano has been doing odd things. We do not know its intent."

The backstory provided no sense of revelation to Rick. He moved on to another line of thought. "What do you want with me?" asked Rick.

Jealousy lingered in silence before responding. "Answers."

"Where are you taking me? Do you expect me to study it for you?"

"You consider yourself a scientist. That all answers come from things observable," said Anger, with a tone that matched his mask.

"I believe the answers I have needed in life I have been able to find on my own strength. Though that doesn't mean I am immune to faith."

"We have watched you change over the years. It is interesting to see you still have some things in common with him," said Hope.

"Who?" asked Rick.

"The one who guides us."

"Who guides you? Where are you taking me?" asked Rick, growing in frustration and fear. The men's persistent prodding prevented him from lingering in protest.

"Our home was peaceful before you arrived. We have watched you change, and with your change our volcano becomes more volatile," said Sadness.

Rick chuckled, "You're not going to sacrifice me, are you?"

The men remained silent.

"Are you?! What good is sacrificing a scientist who could otherwise help you? It will never work. It's a volcano!"

"While your science may discredit our actions, we know that the one who guides us will not betray us. We act on our faith and have what science could never provide us with, hope."

"Who is the one who guides you? Is it Tim?" asked Rick in a growing panic.

"It is the one who recently revealed himself to you. You used to know him well," answered Jealousy.

"He is just using you to get revenge," shouted Rick angrily.

"Our master is not so swayed by emotion as to seek revenge. Our island has changed as you have changed. We simply want to reverse what you have done, the change that you caused," said Hope.

Rick climbed to the opening of the volcano, coerced by the efforts of the men behind him. The air was wavy before him as heat radiated from the magma below, bringing with it a noxious smell stinging his nose and making him lightheaded. The moisture in Rick's skin ripped out in an instant.

17 January 2515

"You said you wanted answers," yelled Rick over the rumbling of the volcano. "You never asked me anything. How is this going to give you answers?"

Hope placed a hand on Rick's shoulder. "You built this world in your mind. It grows and changes in tandem with your development. We are subject to the changes you inflict upon us in the world. The answer we are looking for is if it is possible to purge you from here and bring peace back to our island."

Fear and anger swelled within Rick at the idea that he might be haunted by Tim while he was awake and also asleep. "Tim may think he has me defeated, but this is still my dream. And I'll tell you right now, I've died a hundred times on this island and I always seem to come back here. Killing me now won't provide the answers you are looking for. However, unlike Tim, when I die here I just wake up," and with that he threw himself into the volcano.

20 July 2550
Chapter 37

The air was silent and still as Rick ate his lunch. Linda had long ago refused to talk to him after what she knew he had done to Tim. He hadn't told her directly, but she figured it out and he struggled to deny it when she confronted him. He wasn't sure if Linda had told the rest of the crew, and he didn't much care to find out as long as they remained compliant. He had no interest in having relationships with the rest of the crew because he was no longer sure of how he would behave.

He finished his meal and stood up to put his dishes away. As he turned around he saw the shadowy figure waiting in the distance. As time passed, his feelings for his ever-present incorporeal follower transformed from crippling fear to near apathy to occasional aggression. He had learned to try his best to ignore the shadow, because no matter how hard he tried to lose it, the shadow always followed him. He would, on occasion, still be startled when the apparition would appear, peeking out from a closet or around a dark corner. However, even that had become somewhat predictable and mundane. His guest seemed to naturally linger at a distance, but never fled if Rick approached, nor had he ever displayed any aggression toward Rick. Rick chose to never push his luck. He didn't want to find out what would happen if he interacted with his unwanted visitor. Because of this, the one change he had permanently acquired was to avoid going near the shadow, which is what he was doing now. He needed to go to storage to retrieve replacement kitchen supplies since many of the tools he used were very worn or broken. However, the shadow was near the teleporter so Rick would use the one in the next room instead.

Rick walked into engineering and activated the teleporter. As he stepped on it and turned around, he could see the shadow watching him from a distance. In an instant he was in the storage room, and as he looked out he immediately saw the phantom awaiting his arrival. He recognized the irony that isolation was the biggest threat to the success of the mission, yet with his new companion all he wanted was to be left alone.

"What do you want from me?" yelled Rick to the distant shadow. "Are you Tim? Do you want revenge? You've done nothing! Are you just lingering around me to watch me suffer?" Rick shook his head. "You're not Tim. He wasn't like that. Are you my wraith? Am I a sixteenth century Scott now? Or maybe you're German and you go by Doppelganger instead?" Rick kicked the ground with his right foot in frustration. "You can't be my wraith or doppelganger. You're just a shadow, you don't look like me, and it's been years of you following me and I'm not dead yet. Go away!"

Rick grabbed a pencil out of his pocket and threw it impotently in the direction of the shadow. It fell far short of his target. He stormed to the nearby console and typed in a command to retrieve the kitchen storage container. A large crane attached to the ceiling lurched forward before it whirred to life as it moved to track down its target. Rick could hear it working even as it moved far away.

With seething anger Rick watched the distant apparition. It stood conspicuously in the center of two aisles of containers forty meters away. *Even where he places himself is ambiguous,* thought Rick. *He often stands in the open, only standing in obscured places when space is confined, and he often stands far away. He is not sneaky or confrontational, which might convey aggression. He is never close or standing near anything that might reveal some message or intent. His presence, for years now, has been seemingly purposeless.*

Then, for the first time that Rick had ever noticed, the shadow seemed to move. It started to vibrate, the whole shadow shaking in a slow pulse. Gradually the pulse quickened. Suddenly the shadow that normally stayed still in the distance began to jitter wildly. Shocked by the sudden change, Rick became tense, his muscles tightening in anticipation, as the shadow moved back and forth. It quickly jumped around like examples he had seen in documentaries of VHS tapes having tracking issues. The shape stayed the same, but the position bounced around unpredictably. All of Rick's anger drained from him as fear took over.

A noise overhead pulled Rick's attention as he momentarily looked up to see the crane with the crate above him, unsure if he should wait for it to descend or run away from the suddenly agitated shadow. As Rick looked back at the shadow, he saw it moving toward him at a shockingly quick pace. In an instant of surprise and terror Rick turned around and ran. After a few steps, Rick heard a crack and the squeal of grinding metal. He kept running. Then there was a crash accompanied by a deep vibration in the floor as the crate broke loose from the crane's grip and fell where he had been standing seconds earlier. He turned around and examined the damage to the three by four meter room-sized crate in amazement of his good fortune. He never would have survived being hit by the crate.

In the distance he saw the shadow back where it had been, motionless.

15 October 2600
Chapter 38

Rick gasped for breath as the elliptical he was running on beeped, indicating he had passed the two mile mark. His joints hurt too much to jog anymore, but as arthritis and blindness began setting in, he was desperate to do anything he could to maintain his health. His hairline, now heavily receded, made of purely gray hair. His skin was spotted and wrinkly, and his once large frame, now reduced, all reflected his growing frailty. He was exercising while he waited for results from the blood labs he had taken. He was anxious to receive good news because he knew this would likely be the last time his eye sight would be good enough to read the results.

While he stressed about other aspects of his health deteriorating, he had learned to deal with his approaching blindness. The moment he realized how quickly his eyesight was failing, he began practicing daily tasks with blindfolds on while he still had the ability to check his work. He was now comfortable cooking while blindfolded and had learned all the voice commands he would need to run the ship. He also practiced the sequence for activating the teleporter, for when he arrived at Planet D-173, twice a day.

A soft chiming emanated from his watch, alerting him that his test results would be ready now. He wiped the sweat off his face and put his glasses on. He held the watch close to his face as he fumbled with it to turn the alarm off. Even with his glasses, he struggled to see details on anything that wasn't inches from his eyes.

Throughout the years he became more and more distant from the crew, acknowledging the needlessness of maintaining relationships with them even on the basic level of maintaining the ship. Yet the more he distanced himself from that reality, the closer the shadowy figure came to him. He had no idea who the figure was, though he was sure that it meant him no harm since he was certain the figure had saved his life at least once. While he hoped his companion was Jessica protecting him, he had his doubts since it left him alone and in no way attempted to communicate with him. He no longer dared to try and communicate with the figure in fear that he might upset it, forcing it to abandon him.

Rick walked to medical. In an attempt to force himself to be active, he avoided the teleporters whenever possible. The door to the lab was still open from when he had his blood drawn. He could see lights flashing on a nearby computer that his results were ready. He leaned in as close to the screen as he could get to read the results. All of his labs came back showing normal. He breathed a sigh of relief. He knew his journey was nearing its end and he was glad to know he didn't need to manage medication while being blind.

He walked with as much of a spring in his step as his aged body would allow as he made his way to the docking bay. He knew the comfort he felt would improve the chances of him having a peaceful rest in the sleep chamber. Before heading to the sleep chamber, he would do one last test run of activating the teleporter. As he reached the entrance to the docking bay, he closed his eyes.

He carefully reached out and groped the door frame until he found the rope he had attached to it. The rope led him directly to the console for the teleporter. He didn't want to attempt to navigate the zero-gs of the docking bay unassisted. He then gently felt the console for two buttons, one to turn it on and the other to initiate voice commands. After he found the buttons, placing one under his index finger and the other under his pinky, he peeked to make sure he had it correct. He pretended to press them in order, and then began reciting the voice commands he had read from the manual.

"Computer, activate teleporter unit three, zero, four," he said loudly.

"Teleporter three, zero, four can not be activated until external power is terminated. Terminate external power now?" He rattled off quickly in a high voice.

"Yes, terminate external power now," he replied to himself.

"Please place your hand on the scanner for final confirmation." He then placed his hand on the scanner attached to the console and made a whirring sound as he pretended that it was working. "Confirmation complete, please remove your hand."

"Ding." He made the noise that indicated that the teleporter was now activated.

He paused for a moment.

"Ding." He faked the second sound that indicated that a connection had been established with another teleporter. He did his best to stay positive and ignore the fear that he may never hear that second chime. Instead, he would often distract himself with questions about what language the people who would come through the teleporter might speak, or if English still existed on Earth in any fashion that he could possibly recognize or understand.

"That's enough play time for now, I guess," he said to himself. He then made his way to his home.

Entering his home, he didn't bother turning on the lights. Navigating the space purely from memory, he made his way upstairs and entered his room. He struggled out of his clothing. His shirt, with his diminishing range of motion and missing arm, gave him the most trouble and left him relieved to soon lay down. Lastly, he set his glasses on the corner of his dresser where they would be easy to retrieve, and carefully climbed into his sleep chamber.

Reflecting on the positive results of his health exam, he let out a relieved sigh and smiled to himself. The excitement of nearing the end of his mission filled him with an optimism that had diminished long ago. He thought of Jessica and hoped she was proud of him. Then he closed his eyes.

22 August 2612
Chapter 39

Rick found himself climbing a volcano, surrounded by men in masks, but something seemed different.

"Why are my hands and feet not chained this time? He asked his captors.

"As your health fails you waste less energy on false realities. As you draw nearer to him, we know you are less likely to disobey," said the man behind Rick.

"Draw near to who, the shadowy figure?" asked Rick.

"Yes."

"Who is he? I doubt it's Tim, even though he showed up after I killed Tim. Is it Jason or Matt?"

"They died over two hundred years ago, light years away from where you are now. Do you really think it could be one of them?" asked the man wearing the mask of anger.

"Are you implying that the shadowy figure is no one? Just a part of my imagination?" asked Rick. "He saved my life."

"Did he? Or was it just chance?" asked happiness.

"No, he never acted like that before or after the day he saved my life. He knew what was going to happen." Rick replied forcefully.

Everyone climbed the volcano silently. Rick realized this was the first time he had heard any of the other men speak. He thought about the exchange they just had, what they had said, and how they said it. Then he finally figured out what seemed odd about it. They all had the same voice, one that sounded painfully familiar.

"Who are you?" asked Rick.

"Who are you asking?" replied Fear.

"Any of you. It doesn't matter who. The answer will be the same for all of you!"

"You do not realize the potential depth of your question," said Jealousy. "If you are asking us, we are the emotions divided of the one who guides us. If you are asking our master, he is the one who observes all truth, who leads us based on what is real. If you are asking yourself, you are a lost and desperate man who has built many walls. Yet, as your health fails, those walls come down, and you begin to once again see the truth and draw close to our master."

"Was it necessary to take an easy question and make it so complicated?" snapped Rick.

He put his head down and walked silently. He was frustrated knowing that more questions would likely yield similarly vague answers.

After walking for a few minutes, he tripped on a stone and went crashing to his knees. He paused, kneeling on the ground, and waited for someone to help him up. Two men came to his assistance, lifting him up, one on each side of him. As they stood there helping him, he quickly turned and pulled off the mask of the man to his right.

Rick stood, stunned, as he attempted to digest what he was seeing. As he stared at the young man before him, he became aware of just how much he had aged. For the person was no stranger, but was Rick when he was much younger.

"So you are the emotions, divided, of the one who sees the truth, me?" asked Rick rhetorically. "Or, I guess, of my subconscious?"

"Try not to think of him as your subconscious. You lost your sanity a long time ago, and the divide between conscious and subconscious is pretty much gone. He is the part of you that is still able to distinguish between actual external input, like sight and sound, from those things that your brain completely fabricates," said Sadness.

"As you drift away from the stories, the pictures, the drama, and the depression, as you begin to accept your reality and focus on your goals rather than your guilt, he draws closer," said Anger.

Rick paused, looked down at the dirt and gravel beneath his feet. "So," Rick paused. "The shadowy figure is me, and the volcano is a metaphor for my mission."

Rick looked up. The men were gone and he was alone. For the first time he took a moment to enjoy the island he was climbing. The birds in the trees around him chirped quietly, and the wind was gentle and cool as it passed. The beach in the distance provided a soothing rhythm to accompany the birds. The saltwater and surrounding foliage provided a fresh aroma that he did not realize the stale air of the spaceship lacked until now. He quietly put his head down and continued the climb alone.

He was in better physical shape in his dream than in real life, and he enjoyed the climb. He paused often to enjoy the view. With his new revelation he feared that he would no longer have a reason to revisit the island in his dreams, so he took the time to savor the experience.

As the sun began to set, he wandered off the path he was following to gather some berries for a snack. Finding a comfortable place to sit, he watched the sun go down as the waves crashed on the beach. The moon rose high in the sky and provided much of the light that the sun had given before it set. The light that the moon cast rippled on the water and reflected a brilliant white off of the top of the palm leaves.

When Rick was done resting, he continued his climb. He could tell he was close to the top as the heat around him grew stronger. The smell distinctly changed as he reached the peak of the volcano. He could see a soft glow rising from the lava below. As he reached the crest and prepared to jump in, he turned around for one last view of the island.

As he stood there silently, he could hear the noises of night life. The crickets provided a symphony of music. He inhaled deeply in an attempt to soak in the moment to its fullest one last time. Then, as a farewell to a place that provided him both fear and growth, he exhaled and fell backwards into the volcano.

01 August 2634
Chapter 4o

Rick awoke in the sleep chamber. As he opened his eyes and attempted to look around, he saw nothing but complete darkness. It was the moment he had been waiting for. He was blind. The health of his eyes seemed to deteriorate faster when in the sleep chamber. He exited the sleep chamber and slowly walked to the dresser in front of him. When he reached it, he took the journal out of his back pocket and set it on the dresser. He wouldn't need it anymore. The lack of visual noise allowed him to feel calm, and the feeling that he was being watched by his shadowy companion was gone. He once again felt entirely alone.

"Computer, relay ship status."

The computer responded over the intercom. "Ship status: all clear. Engine temperature: normal. Hull integrity: normal. Vegetation: normal. Consumption..."

He heard the computer voice for the first time with a new level of clarity. The timbre seemed natural enough, but it contained a synthetic quality he couldn't quite pinpoint. The delivery seemed authentic, but he noticed what he could only describe as digital grit, some level of imperfection indistinguishable when distracted with his other senses. Rick ignored the computer as it went on. His attention was drawn to his pain. His joints were stiff and his left knee was filled with a dull ache. He could bear his weight on it when he walked, but he knew that without a cane his use of that knee wouldn't last long.

"Teleporter, destination: Medical," he said as he hobbled his way onto the teleporter.

Upon arrival he paused and tried to remember where the teleporter was in relation to where he was going. Once he remembered the environment, he turned left toward the medical supplies. Reaching the appropriate room, he stood at the entrance, and lingered as frustration struck him. He couldn't remember what the room looked like, and had no idea where the canes would be.

"Why didn't I think of this before I was blind?" He said angrily. "I knew this day was coming!"

He took a deep breath and tried to shake his anger as he spoke to himself calmly. "I didn't know my knee was going to hurt the day I went blind and I would need a cane. There is no reason that I should have grabbed one before now," he reassured himself. "I'll just take my time and search carefully. It's not like I have anything else I need to do."

He slowly followed the wall to his right, carefully favoring his aching knee, hoping the canes were standing nearby. He shuffled his feet along the floor to avoid tripping and gently bumped into shelves, hearing things hit the ground around him. When he reached the back of the room with his searching hands, he heard the light clatter of sticks, and felt a bundle of canes leaning in the corner. Triumphant relief seized him. He grabbed as many as he could carry, in case he ever lost one, and exited the room.

. . .

Rick cautiously set his hand in a drawer and slowly

moved his fingers around to feel for the fork that he wanted while delicately avoiding the knives. While he was grateful that he had taught himself to cook blind, he did not realize how much he had cheated. Cooking with only one hand was hard, but doing so while blind felt impossible. He often allowed himself to settle for raw ingredients rather than complex meals, though even that came with unforeseen challenges. He had not prepared himself for how little he would recognize many things simply through feeling.

Anything contained in a bottle or jar, especially if the seal was too tight, became a nearly insurmountable challenge that rarely rewarded him with the desired ingredient. His efforts often resulted in minutes of struggle and a potential mess, only to give the item a sniff and realize it wasn't what he had wanted. He often reminded himself that happiness was a luxury far removed from the survival he was so focused on.

"Computer, time remaining until destination arrival?" asked Rick.

"Estimated time of arrival in one year, three months, and twelve days," replied the computer.

"Computer, resume audio book."

A soothing male voice resumed reading *The Gunslinger* by Stephen King. Audio books were one of the only ways he knew how to pass the time, and the comfort he received from being talked to was his only method to fend off the loneliness that he battled against now that he couldn't be consumed by his imaginary world revolving around his pictures. His day, now solely focused on maintaining his body until the ship's arrival, was limited to eating, exercising, and audio books. Any effort to maintain the ship had been dropped out of fear of injury.

Rick ate a simple pasta he had made as he allowed himself to be transported to the imaginary world that the narrator described for him. No longer able to abandon reality through his own creations, he now consumed his thoughts with the fiction of others and waited until he could reenter the sleep chamber and speed up the arrival of the ship.

19 September 2635
Chapter 41

Matt swore to himself silently. "The storage space wasn't made to hold this many panels. It's going to be a tight fit to make this work."

"Luckily we have enough anchors to unload all the panels for team one and don't need to go back and forth to drop off panels. That's going to save a ton of time," said Linda.

Matt moved the final panel into the shuttle and closed the doors to the storage area. "All done," he said triumphantly.

"Just in time because the ship should be at a stop soon," said Adelina.

As she spoke the remaining crew members entered the docking bay, followed by Rick.

"Is the shuttle ready?" asked Rick.

"Yes, sir. All the panels have been placed in shuttle one," responded Matt.

"Good. I want the engines to be as warm as possible when we fire them back up, so let's make this quick. Just remember..." Rick paused for a moment.

"Remember what? Is everything okay?" asked Jessica, concerned.

"Uh, yeah, remember that, um, quality matters most, so take the time you need to do the job right," said Rick with a visible look of concern.

"Yes, sir," responded the crew in unison.

Jessica moved close to Rick. "Are you sure you are okay?

What's bothering you?"

"Yeah, I'm alright. I just had the strangest feeling like I've done this before. Just be careful, something doesn't feel right," he replied quietly to Jessica. "Alright, Tim and Jason, take charge of your teams and get this done. The ship will be stopped by the time you are ready in the shuttle. I will monitor your progress from the cockpit, and be careful," said Rick.

"Let's buckle in and get this show on the road," said Tim.

The crew began entering the shuttle and taking their seats. Tim made his way to the driver's seat.

"We'll stop and drop off the heat panels first and then move to the other section of the ship to replace the other panels. There are less heat panels to replace, but they take longer to install. We should be able to knock out our four panels before you finish your three," said Tim to Jason.

"Sounds like a plan," replied Jason.

The shuttle lurched forward as the engine came to life. Tim released the locking mechanism and the shuttle floated up effortlessly.

Rick's chest beat furiously as he watched the shuttle begin to move. He turned on his radio and tuned it to Jessica's frequency. "Please be careful while you're out there. Let me know if anything seems wrong while you're working, okay?"

"I will. Just keep an eye on us from the cockpit and everything will be okay. If you see anything that is off, just tell me what to do and I'll do it," reassured Jessica.

. . .

Rick watched from the cockpit as the shuttle arrived at its first stop and the crew began removing the heat panels. It took nearly ten minutes to remove each panel and anchor them to the ship. The anchors were long enough that the panels could be maneuvered into place without worrying about them floating away. As the crew began moving the first panel into place, the other two floated peacefully.

Tim fired his side thrusters to turn the shuttle so that he could fire the rear exhaust away from the three crew members outside of the shuttle. Rick could tell that the shuttle was difficult to steer. Tim was close to the panels and fired his side thrusters to try and avoid them. As Rick watched, a panel shot forward.

"Watch it!" yelled Jason.

"You shouldn't have pinned me in!" Snapped Tim as he gunned it before the panel had a chance to block him again.

"Status report now! What's that white stuff coming off the shuttle?" questioned Rick.

Jason moved to the panel that had been hit and examined it. "Everything looks fine. Luckily, these things are really strong. From here it looks like the white particles from the shuttle are paint chips. No noticeable damage that I can see."

Rick's chest began to beat painfully. "I don't like this at all," said Rick.

Tim flew the ship to its next destination and the crew began removing the first panel. Yellow caution lights on the screen in front of Rick turned to red as the two teams removed the original panels. When Tim's team had finished replacing their first panel, a red light turned green. Rick looked to see Jason's team finish their first panel as well.

"The computer says we are green for the first heat panel.

Looks like you nailed it with the fabrication," said Rick.

"We have good tools, so I was never too concerned, but it is a relief," replied Jason.

One by one the yellow lights in front of Rick turned red and then green. Tim, Linda, and Jessica had just begun returning to the other team as the last heat panel finished installation and the control panel gave a green light.

"All panels have been successfully installed. Let's bring it in so we can fire this ship back up," said Rick.

"Jason, when we get back to the ship we are going to have to take a look at the shuttle. The panel must have done more damage than we can see because the left side jets don't seem to be firing very well and acceleration is slow," said Tim.

"Sounds like a fuel line is pinched, probably nothing major. You're almost here. I'll take a quick look before I get on board," replied Jason.

Rick's stomach knotted up immediately. He knew something significant was wrong.

"Tell me if you see the left jets firing in a second, when I turn," said Tim.

"Tim," chimed Rick nervously. "Now is not a good time to diagnose a problem with the shuttle. You're floating outside of the ship. It's a dangerous spot to be troubleshooting."

Tim and Jason were too distracted to acknowledge Rick. The radio was quiet for a few seconds as Rick watched the shuttle on his monitor.

"See anything?" asked Tim.

"No, and it doesn't look like you are turning. See anything different from your angle, Rick?" asked Jason.

"Just a little flicker from your thrusters. If it is a pinched fuel line than maybe you just have to give it a bit more gas," replied Rick almost instinctively. He felt wrong saying it and quickly tried to correct himself. "No wait, don't do that. Just get back safely. It's too dangerous out there."

"Let's see what happens," said Tim, not acknowledging Rick's warning.

"No!" shouted Rick.

Again, the crew didn't acknowledge him.

Rick changed the radio to Jessica's frequency. "Jessica, can you hear me?" Rick's voice was filled with urgency.

"Yes, are you okay?"

"Jessica, something bad is about to happen."

"What do you mean? Because of the pinched fuel line?"

"It's not a pinched fuel line. It's a leak. It's going to explode if he gives it more gas!"

Rick watched the screen helplessly, waiting, overwhelmed with the feeling that he knew what would happen. The thrusters lit up more than the previous attempt and then quickly went dark.

"What happened? It felt like it was working and then cut out," said Tim.

Looking closely, Rick noticed mist coming from the dent in the shuttle.

"Jessica, move away from the thrusters!" Rick banged on the console in front of him, knowing what was about to happen and unable to do anything about it.

"I'll try giving it more..."

"No!" screamed Rick. "Cut the engines!"

A quick flash of orange shot out, licking up the gas that had escaped. Just as quickly as it had shot out it was sucked back in and a small explosion instantly threw the shuttle into a spin toward the crew outside. Rick could hear Jessica and Linda screaming over the radio.

Matt was shouting at Adelina to get out of the way as he attempted to push her before the shuttle hit them both. The shuttle was moving too quickly to escape, but before it hit them a second explosion ripped the shuttle in half. Rick knew it had killed Matt and Adelina instantly.

Tim, who had been closest inside the shuttle to the explosion, flew out in multiple pieces, his blood crystallizing as it hit space.

Linda's mask had been fractured and Rick saw her grasping at her mask momentarily until she finally went limp.

Jason and Taisha had been thrown by the explosion into the ship. Rick could see gas escaping from a canister on Taisha's hip that he knew was oxygen. She began searching for more oxygen, but the bodies she could reach were too destroyed and the shuttle had moved too far away for her to reach it. Jason had hit the ship on his back, which made the jet pack on his back explode. The explosion threw him into space, unable to slow his speed and return to the ship. His arms waived wildly as he desperately reached for the ship that moved farther and farther away from him.

The radio was filled with static as Rick watched the screens in front of him, knowing there was nothing he could do.

The radio cracked. "Rick," said Jessica softly.

"Jessica! Are you okay? I don't see you." Rick desperately searched the screen for any sign of her.

"I moved to the other side of the shuttle, like you told me

to."

"Are you okay?"

"I can't move my legs. I was thrown by the explosion and I think I broke them."

"I'm coming for you, sweetie. Just hold tight and I'll get you!"

"Rick," she said so calmly that it made him pause. "The other shuttle is broken. There is no way for you to get to me without killing yourself."

He refused to admit the truth behind what she said. He began to scramble to find a solution. "Don't give up, I can bring you back!" Rick's voice cracked as tears began streaming down his face. Desperation flooded him as he struggled to find hope. "I can still help you."

"Rick," she repeated with the same calmness that once again gave him pause. "I don't need you to help me. I need you to talk to me."

Rick choked as he fought back tears. "I have to save you. I need you with me."

"No matter how hard you try, there is nothing you can do to bring me back. This isn't your fault. We all made choices that led to this moment. You can't blame yourself."

"I am supposed to be the leader and I let this happen. No one can take the blame for this other than me."

"You can't do this to yourself. A true leader doesn't rule with an iron fist. He lets those around him do what they do best. Sometimes mistakes happen, but people perform better when they feel like they have control, when their heart is in it because they own their own actions. You know this. This is what you let us do. We voted on it through our actions. It wasn't your fault."

"But I can't do this without you," whispered Rick. "You already have."

30 September 2635
Chapter 42

"Ship deceleration, initiated. Estimated arrival in six weeks, three days, seventeen hours."

Rick struggled to comprehend what he heard as he awoke in his sleep chamber. He fought through extreme pain as he attempted to escape his mechanical cocoon. His muscles were so atrophied that he collapsed to the floor upon his exit. His chest heaved in and out as he desperately attempted to get to his feet.

It had been his fear of dying that had tempted him to use the sleep chamber despite his rapidly diminishing health, and he was now afraid that decision could be what cost him the mission. He crawled to a nearby cane and tried to pull himself to his feet. He still did not have the strength.

"Computer, reduce gravity to fifty percent."

His breathing lightened as gravity lessened. He pulled himself to his feet. Every muscle in his body hurt like a waking limb. Yet after waiting several minutes, the pain did not go away.

"I spent too much time in the sleep chamber. I've caused permanent damage," he said to himself. "I'm never going to last six weeks."

. . .

Slowly the minutes passed by, turning into hours, days,

and eventually weeks. As time crawled forward, Rick grew weaker and weaker. To compensate, he kept lowering the gravity until it was entirely off. No time period had felt as long to him as the past five weeks. He spent most of his time listening to audio books and trying to figure out the chance that anyone would come through the teleporter when he activated it.

He usually stayed floating near the fruit and vegetables dispenser. Without gravity he could not cook without losing most of his food, so he ate the ingredients raw. He chose to rarely leave where he was so he wouldn't get lost, and to exert himself as little as possible. The pain he was in left him unable to control his sleep. He would fall asleep only when his fatigue outweighed his pain, then struggle to reorient himself after drifting away from where he normally stayed. His life of anxiety and pain was only interrupted by the extreme intestinal pain that his limited diet caused him. One agonizing torment momentarily replaced by another every time he attempted to use the restroom.

He couldn't help but laugh at the miserable corpse he would be greeting his earthly visitors with if he were successful.

...

"Secure all belongings and sit in cockpit chairs with safety restraints tightened. Landing to commence in five minutes," announced the computer.

Rick struggled to get to a nearby teleporter. "Computer, go to the cockpit," said Rick as he entered the teleporter. He coughed fiercely after he spoke and could taste blood. He had been fighting an extreme fever for several days and was relieved that his arrival meant he could stop worrying about dying soon.

Rick searched helplessly to find a chair in the cockpit. He immediately became disoriented, floating in the open until he slammed his shoulder into a wall. He reached out frantically until he found a chair. Adrenaline kept him from noticing most of his pain, but it didn't stop his hand from shaking violently as he attempted to fasten his restraints.

He finished his seat belt as the computer announced, "Optimal landing zone discovered. Turbulence, mild, air temperature, thirty-five point six degrees Celsius, humidity, thirty-four percent. Now entering the atmosphere."

As the ship shook and gravity set in, Rick could feel his lungs burning from the strain. The noise around him thundered in his ears as they popped repeatedly during the descent. He began to panic as he realized that even as the ship dropped the gravity was too much for him to move. His muscles had atrophied too much from zero-gravity and age. He began to fear that he would die, unable to lift himself out of his seat.

"Now lowering the landing gear."

For the past four weeks Rick had been worried about the landing gear failing as it was the one part of the ship that was never tested. Yet now that the moment had come, he didn't even notice that the ship was about to land. He knew he was too weak to move and gravity alone might kill him.

The ship bounced up and down as it tried to control its descent. Rick's head shook around, his neck too weak to fight the turbulence. Finally, the ship landed with a thud and his head was thrown back into the chair, knocking him out.

15 November 2635

Chapter 43

Rick awoke to the sound of waves crashing in the distance. The sun shone in his eyes as it broke over the horizon. Sand seeped between his fingers as he sat himself up. The familiar environment of a thousand dreams brought a sense of comfort despite the number of nightmares he had here.

"I was afraid I was never going to see you again," said Jessica as she added more sticks to a nearby fire, the silhouette of her face outlined by the nearby flames. "You were gone for so long."

"Did I die?" asked Rick, his voice weak as though from a long slumber.

"No, you just hit your head," said Jessica as she came over and kissed his forehead. "You'll wake up soon."

Rick shook his head. "I can't do it," he said with remorse.

"Yes, you can. You've made it this far. You're almost done." She grabbed his hand, which looked worn and tired next to her still young skin, and helped him to his feet. "I managed to kill some birds for breakfast, but I haven't gotten any other food yet. I'm pretty sure I found some fruit back when we were gathering firewood previously. How about, you help me collect some food for breakfast?"

Rick suppressed all the emotions he was feeling and the things he wanted to say to Jessica and simply complied with her request. For half an hour they collected various berries they found and then returned to their camp. Rick's body slowly gained more energy and strength, revitalized by Jessica's presence. Her body moved with the same grace that it always had.

As they started to eat the food that Jessica had prepared Rick began to weep openly.

"I don't want to leave you again," he said between gasps of breath.

"It will be okay. We will have our time together soon enough," she replied sweetly. Her brilliant green eyes pierced his heart, flooding him with a desire to remain with her. "You're almost done."

"But I can't do it."

"Yes you can, honey."

"No, literally. I can't do it. I am too weak to go on. I've been living with the gravity off for too long to be able to make my way out of the cockpit."

"You made it this far, didn't you? You beat the odds and did something that even you thought, at times, was impossible. How is this any different? You just have to find the fuel that will drive you to the end."

"What if I make it to the machine and turn it on and no one is there to activate the other teleporter?"

"Since when is that your responsibility? How Earth is doing and whether anyone comes through that teleporter is not your problem. Don't become defeated over things you have no control over. Is your mission a failure if you turn on the teleporter and no one comes through, or is their mission a failure for not holding up their end of the bargain?"

Rick ate his breakfast quietly, his emotions too strong to be dismissed as quickly as Jessica had diffused his arguments.

Finally, after a long silence, "How do I get the strength to overcome what is ahead of me?" His faded blue eyes looked at her in desperation, begging for guidance.

"I can't tell you that, because I don't know," replied Jessica as she finished her meal and stood up. She turned to him and helped him to his feet. "Let's just enjoy the time we have left."

They walked along the beach for a while. Rick remained deep in thought. Jessica clung to him, her body pressed against his arm.

"Staying here with me is not going to help you anymore," said Jessica. "You have an issue before you that you can't run from, you can't ignore, and you can't put it off."

"You said I have to find what fuels me, but I don't know what it is. You got me this far, but now my desire to be with you outweighs my will to persevere. I would rather give up and be with you."

Jessica turned to face Rick, grabbed both his hands and gave them a tight squeeze. She looked at him with conviction. He struggled to look into the eyes that he had loved for so long as they pushed him beyond what he felt capable of. "I can't be your driving force now, but you will have your rest soon enough. Why did you keep going? Why do you care to finish this at all? Is it your pride? Honor? You are the only one to solve this and you have to solve it quickly because your time here is up."

15 November 2635
Chapter 44

"Oxygen levels, normal. Carbon dioxide, low. Ship status... Hull, intact. Engines, offline."

Rick ignored the computer as it continued to read off statistics. He struggled to lift his arm off the arm rest. After lifting it several inches, he let his arm collapse onto his lap. He was relieved that his hand fell onto the latch he needed to press to release his seat belt. However, his hand was too weak to press the button hard enough to release his straps. He fought with it for several minutes until he tried lifting his other arm and dropping it on his hand as he desperately pushed on the button. The force was just enough to release his straps.

As he removed his straps, he slid down to the floor and lay on his back. His chest heaved as he strained for breath. His exertion out of his chair made him cough, which brought the taste of blood back to his mouth and made his lungs burn. His heart ached as though he had just run a mile. He clutched at his chest, writhing on the floor in pain. Then a calmness swept over him as he struggled for breath. For the first time he felt the bones of his chest. Rubbing his hands together, he noticed how frail they were. He had spent his whole life trying to survive and in an instant it was gone. Yet despite his efforts, he was about to die on the doorstep of what he had striven for; what he had told himself was his destiny.

He desperately thought about what Jessica had told him, to find what fueled him, but he couldn't overcome his pain and find an answer. He wept loudly as he thought about how lonely he had been, suffering for an event that he wouldn't get to fulfill. His sacrifice was for nothing. Then suddenly, he felt a new pain as he dwelled on the thought of sacrifice. He was instantly filled with the memory of Jessica dying, with a vividness he hadn't experienced since the day it had happened.

With a strengthened resolve, he flipped onto his stomach and fought to pull himself forward. Inch by inch he found chairs, computer consoles, and walls to pull and kick his way to the docking bay. His heart raged in his chest under the strain. His arms and legs felt like a thousand needles stabbing him with each push forward.

As he reached the hallway that connected the cockpit to the docking bay, he collapsed. His heart was in excruciating pain and his left arm was numb. He knew he was having a heart attack and only had a few minutes to activate the teleporter before he would be dead. This realization gave him fear so strong that it overpowered his pain. He continued forward until he could just barely reach the teleporter's console while lying on the ground. Clutching at the console, he managed to turn it on and activate voice commands.

"Computer, activate teleporter unit three, oh, four," he said quietly.

"Command unclear," replied the computer.

Rick gasped for breath. "Computer," he said while panting, "activate teleporter unit three, oh, four!"

"Teleporter three, zero, four can not be activated until

external power is..."

"Terminate... terminate external power!" Rick coughed as he interrupted the computer.

The computer stopped speaking abruptly. Rick waited.

"Please place your hand on the scanner for final confirmation."

With one final push of his will, he forced himself up onto his amputated arm so he could reach the scanner. He screamed in agony as he held his hand on the scanner. Finally he fell back to the floor and clutched his chest.

"Confirmation complete, please remove your hand."

As the computer spoke it sounded distant to Rick. He suddenly felt detached from his pain and for the first time in several years he saw a light. His body was cold, and just as he was about to be embraced by the light, he snapped back to attention as he heard a noise.

Ding.

He remembered what the sound meant, the teleporter was active. He had done it, completed his part of the mission. But just as the sound brought him back to the situation at hand, it also brought back the pain.

"I just need to hear the second chime... to know they activated their teleporter," he said to himself.

With each moment that he waited, his pain grew uncontrollably. "Please let someone be there, please," he cried desperately. "There has to be someone, anyone."

When he could no longer bear the pain, he breathed deeply and thought about Jessica. As he exhaled he was consumed by the light.

Ding.

Acknowledgments

This book would not exist in its current form without the unbelievable help of the three who read the draft and provided invaluable feedback. My mom, Diane Rice, you are the first to have given me feedback and your encouragement drove me forward, washing away the doubts and insecurities that always plague me with any of my art. My grandfather, Keith Aldridge, your focus on the science within my book (among other things) was extremely helpful and eye opening to gaps I had struggled with within my story telling. My wife, Julie Jaeger, you support me in enough ways that they would require their own book to list, you are my Jessica. To the three of you, I hope that I have put your time and effort to good use and produced something that you can be proud to have been a part of. Thank you!

Steven Jaeger

was born outside of Chicago in 1985. He spent his formative years in Arizona. He is a devout guitar player and drummer. He currently resides in Oregon with his lovely wife of eighteen years and three children, who he expects to surpass him in greatness soon. He has a BA in Game Design and has spent the majority of his career building imaginary things for the internet. He is now spending his spare time writing imaginary things for you.

Made in the USA
Las Vegas, NV
16 June 2022